DISCORD AND CINDER

FIRE WITCHES OF SALEM
BOOK SEVEN

CARRIE PULKINEN

CHAPTER I
CINDER

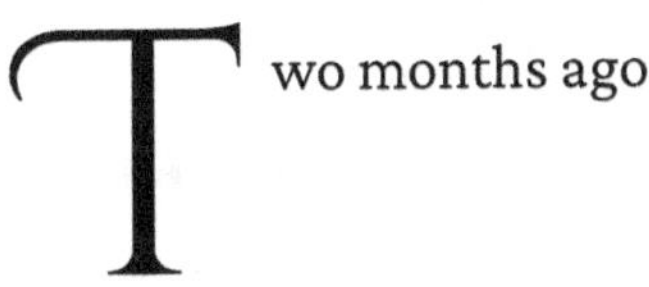wo months ago

---

Dear Ash,

If you're reading this, I never made it back.

I know you planned to organize the library in Dad's absence, so I hid your favorite sigil book next to this journal in hopes that you'd find it should I go missing too. I really did leave in search of our parents. I didn't lie about that, but there are other things you need to know. You and Ember.

Our parents lied to you about the curse. They lied to us all. Every High Priestess that came before

Mom lied too. You aren't the miracle baby she made you out to be. There's a reason why you're the only third daughter to survive.

Mom didn't have the heart to kill you.

The curse wasn't that every third daughter of the High Priestess would die in infancy. It was that she would go insane and murder everyone in the coven.

I know it's hard to believe, but Mom showed me the curse. It was in the dark grimoire in the safe.

The dirty secret of our coven is that if the High Priestess has a third daughter, she murders her. It has happened several times over the centuries, and the knowledge about the real curse is passed orally from the High Priestess to her oldest daughter. That's why I now know.

Mom has been searching for a way to break the curse since you were born. She was certain she'd figured out how to end it for good without harming you. The witch who hexed us harnessed the power of three demons, and only three demons can break the curse.

Mom and Dad went into the woods to summon one. They cut a deal with him. I overheard them talking about it. They promised their souls in exchange for him delivering the fiends responsible. The demon required the grimoire, so they took it back to the woods, but the one they bargained with was a trickster. He took the book and our parents, but not before I tore out the page identifying the only demons who could break the curse. The ones who created it.

The witch who cursed us moved to Boston and joined the Magic Society there. I broke into their library, and that's where I discovered what she had done. She had promised her own soul and her first-born's in exchange for the power, but she never planned to hold up her end of the deal.

She vanquished the three demon brothers but hid their skulls. Without their bodies intact, they can't reform in Hell. They're trapped in a dark prison and never got to collect her soul. The only way to break the curse is for us to release them. They are the only ones who can help.

I've located Discord's skull, and I'm going to release him. I'll convince him to take me into Hell so I can find Mom and Dad. I hope to bring them back right away, so you never have to read this, but if I don't return, you have to release the other two. We can end this. I know we can.

Love, Cinder

My hand shook as I scrawled my name at the bottom of the page. Every word I'd written was true, but I never dreamed I'd have to write it down. To not only drag the morbid skeletons from my family's closet and dance with them, but to record the evidence for anyone's prying eyes to see.

That's why I planned to hide the journal where only Ash could find it. If anyone else discovered what my ancestors had been doing all these years—what Ash was destined to do if we didn't stop the curse—they'd destroy us. They'd have no other choice.

"Hey." Chrys knocked on my open door, making me jump. "Everything okay?"

"Yeah. Why wouldn't it be?" I forced a smile and slipped the journal into my nightstand drawer before sliding it closed and resting my hand on the surface.

"I texted you twice and called when you didn't reply." She stepped into my bedroom and leaned against the doorjamb, tucking her jet-black hair behind her ear. She wore black jeans and a midnight blue sweater that made her eyes pop.

"We're supposed to see a band tonight, remember?" She raised her brows, a sly smile pulling up one corner of her mouth. "Patrice is going to introduce me to the bass player."

"Right. I'm supposed to play wing woman. Sorry, my phone must be on vibrate." I drummed my fingers on the nightstand, contemplating how much to tell her. Chrys was my closest friend. She knew me better than anyone, and I could tell by the look on her face that she knew something was wrong.

"It might be good to get your mind off things." She sank onto the bed next to me and bumped my shoulder with hers. "Take a break from your worries."

I sighed, tilting my head toward the ceiling. "I can't tonight. I... I'm going away for a while."

She shifted her weight, curling her right leg beneath her left and angling toward me. "Your parents again?"

I nodded. "I found another lead."

"Are you leaving tonight? I'll go with you." She tugged her phone from her back pocket. "I'll just let Patrice—"

"No." I shot to my feet. "You've got a bass player ready to finger your strings. Go have fun."

She shrugged. "He can finger me another time. If my bestie is chasing feral fowl, I want to be there. You need to stop isolating yourself, Cin. It's not healthy."

I paced to the closet and opened the door. "I have to do this alone."

She returned the phone to her pocket. "No, you don't."

"Believe me, I do." I grabbed a backpack and laid it on my dresser. "It's a dangerous place, and I won't risk another coven member's life on my 'wild goose chases.'"

"I didn't mean..." She sighed and rose to her feet. "I'm not afraid of a little danger. Besides, what could be more perilous than downtown Salem on Halloween night? All those tourists who suddenly think they're witches, packing into every restaurant and bar in town." She exaggerated a shudder. "It's a nightmare."

"I'm serious." I shoved some pants and two shirts into my bag before throwing in a pair of undies. I bit my lip and grabbed two more pairs...just in case.

"I am too." She rested her hand on my shoulder. "If this place is as dangerous as you say, then you'll need backup. Let me help you."

"I'll be fine." I shrugged off her touch and grabbed a set of knives from my drawer. "It'll probably turn out to be nothing, just like my other leads."

Yes, that was a lie, but best friend or not, I couldn't tell her I had used dark magic to bind myself to a demon, much less that I planned to summon him, follow him to Hell, and fight my way back out again. She'd call on the roots from the nearest tree and tie me to the ground before she'd let me do something that stupid.

She narrowed her eyes, staring at me intently. "You're doing it, aren't you? That fake confidence thing? I swear you could convince Hecate that *you're* the mother of magic if you wanted to."

"Shh." I glanced into the hall and lowered my

voice, speaking through clenched teeth. "It's not fake. It's magic, and I told you that in confidence."

"And you promised never to use it on me." She crossed her arms.

"I'm not. I swear." I drew an X over my heart. "If you're convinced to let me do this alone, it's because you know me well enough to understand I won't do it any other way."

Persuasive magic was a powerful ability that blurred the line between light and dark. I only ever used it passively, making myself appear confident, in control, like I knew exactly what I was doing, even when I didn't. I never dared affect another's free will, nor would I ever.

Chrys was the only person who even knew I had this power, and I never should have confided in her. People got weird when they knew someone could manipulate their decisions with magic. Go figure.

She dropped her arms to her sides, her features softening. "I know you've always been independent, but since your parents disappeared, you've given hard-headed a whole new meaning. Will you at least tell me the general vicinity of where you're going in case you end up missing too?"

I opened my mouth to give her a vague response, but every smoke alarm in the house screeched in unison, saving me from adding another layer of lies.

"Sorry," Ash called from the kitchen.

I closed my eyes for a long blink. "Let me check on her."

My boots thudded on the hardwood as I strode down the hall and crossed the living room, passing a bookcase filled with candles and totems. My youngest sister stood in the kitchen, her blue hair tied in a knot on top of her head as she dumped an entire bag of flour into a fiery skillet on the stove.

"They weren't kidding when they labeled this 'all-purpose.'" She fanned the smoke away from her face and turned toward me. "You should've seen the flame I shot from my fingertip. It was the biggest one yet."

"Ash." I tilted my head and padded toward her, taking her shoulders in my hands. "You know you're not supposed to use your fire magic unsupervised."

"You were right down the hall." She moved the skillet to a cool burner and dragged the trash can toward the stove. "Besides, the grease was the problem. If I'd tried to light the stove before I set the skillet down, it would have been fine."

"You still have to be careful. We might be fireproof, but our house isn't." And it was time to refresh the binding spell Mom had cast on her. The last thing I needed was for her to burn the entire city to the ground before I could get back with our parents.

A pang of guilt stabbed my chest. Our mom had been binding Ash's fire magic since she was little, trying to stop the curse from coming to fruition. It would be easy for a deranged witch to go on a killing spree if fire were hers to command, so we tempered it. Well, Mom did until she disappeared. She'd shown me the spell when she told me about the curse, making me promise to keep Ash's magic at bay if anything were to happen to her.

So, once every six months, Mom made sure my sweet little sister had the self-esteem of a hairless mole rat. Now it was my turn, and my stomach soured at the thought. I could only imagine what it felt like to grow up thinking you were defective. To watch your sisters' powers grow while yours misfired every time you tried to use them.

"You'd think I'd know better by now. This is ruined." She dumped the contents of the skillet into the trash. "I'll order a pizza as soon as Ember gets home."

I glanced toward the hallway, making sure Chrys wasn't within earshot. "I need you to go downstairs and set up for some sigil magic. I'm following another lead tonight."

"What lead? How did you find it?" She set the pan in the sink and rested her hands on her hips.

"It's better if I don't say." I lowered my voice. "I'll need speed and strength, as usual. And immunity to poison. Fast healing, and how's your work on the protection sigil coming along?"

"I think I've mastered it." She crossed her arms.

"Tell me you're taking Ember with you this time, or Chrys at least. Someone who can fight."

I smiled softly and tucked an errant strand of hair behind her ear. "I plan to negotiate, not fight."

"Cinder..."

"You know I can hold my own if it comes down to that." I pressed my lips together, holding her gaze until she sighed heavily.

"Fine. Give me fifteen minutes to clean this mess and get set up." She turned to the sink and scrubbed the pan.

"Thank you, Ash. You're the best."

She let out a dry laugh and shook her head, and I returned to my bedroom, where Chrys still sat on my bed.

"You don't have to do this alone." She squeezed her hands into fists. "The whole team should be helping to find your parents."

She was right. They should be helping, and if I wasn't certain my parents were in Hell because they'd summoned a demon, I'd have the entire coven searching every hidey hole and dark witch's lair within three hundred miles.

But I *was* certain, and it was imperative that no one else found out.

"I need to do this alone. Please let me." I looked into her eyes, asking her to let her friend leap head-first into a danger the rest of the coven could never fathom. "If it doesn't pan out, I'll loop you in on the next one."

She rose, her gaze saying she wasn't convinced. "Cinder…"

"Hingham." I rested my hand on her back, gently pushing her toward the door. "Hingham is the general vicinity of my lead. Now, please go have fun with Patrice and your bass player. Let go of *your* worries for a little while."

She pursed her lips. "Fine. But if you die, I'm hiring a necromancer to bring you back to life so I can kill you myself."

I laughed. "I would expect nothing less."

"Call me if you need backup." She paced down the hall, and I waited until the door clicked shut to take the journal with my letter from my nightstand drawer.

I lifted my mattress and slipped it and Ash's favorite sigil book beneath. Two bottled spells, which I'd mixed while Ash was at the store, sat in my drawer, and I uncorked the one filled with purple powder.

I set my intention and sprinkled it over the mattress. "Heavy weight, keep this object in place. Don't lift or move until my spell is removed."

Magic gathered in the core of my being, tightening my muscles until I sent it outward, onto the bed. I gave the mattress a push, but it didn't budge. I couldn't lift it either. Good. Now no one would accidentally come across what I'd hidden beneath.

Next up was the most powerful cloaking spell I had ever cast. Should I not return, I couldn't chance Ember or another coven member using a spell to find clues about what happened. I could easily see my middle sister taking matters into her own hands and going after the demons herself. With her hot temper, she'd either vanquish them before they could lift the curse or she'd piss them off and get herself killed. I couldn't let that happen.

If my plan didn't work, Ember would become High Priestess and Ash would need to know what she was cursed to become. They'd need each other for balance. Ash could temper Ember's impulsiveness long enough to complete the quest. She'd have to.

"The stronger the magic, the more likely you'll be the only one who can break it, little sis. This is for you." I took a deep breath and uncorked the next potion. "My shroud is strong and stings like bees. Cloak this room from all who seek, except for Ash and her magical sleuth. Only she can discover the truth."

My magic built, fire coursing through my veins as the spell swirled within my psyche. I let it grow until nausea churned in my gut and the hoagie I'd had for lunch threatened to make a reappearance. My head throbbed, pressure expanding in my skull, making it feel like it was about to crack open.

"As I will it, so mote it be." I flung the powdered potion into the air, and magical gray smoke billowed above me, stretching downward to engulf my entire bedroom. All the air in my lungs came out in a rush, and I bent, resting my hands on my knees and dragging in a breath.

"Holy mother of magic." The spell was stronger than I'd thought it would be, but that's what I got for dabbling in magic so gray that it bordered on dark. Hopefully Ash would look for the sigil book the human way and wouldn't try too hard to remove the cloak. This spell would fight back.

I raked in another breath and straightened. It would take at least an hour to recover from casting a spell that strong. Thankfully, Hingham was a ninety-minute drive from Salem. I would be good as new by the time I reached Discord's skull, and thank the goddess for that. I doubted Isabel, the witch who cursed my bloodline, would make it easy to acquire.

With my plan in place, I rummaged through my sock drawer and found Mom's sachet of powder for the magic-binding spell. I finished packing and slung my backpack over my shoulder before heading to the kitchen, where I poured tequila into two glasses and dumped the powder into one.

Swirling the glass to mix it, I headed downstairs and found Ash in her sigil studio, pouring magical ink into a well. She set her tattoo machine on the table next to her other supplies and spun around to face me.

"Let me grab—" She lowered her brow as her gaze

locked on the glasses. "Tell me you're not drinking before you head out on a magical quest."

"We both are." I offered her the tainted glass. "Do a shot of liquid courage with me. This one could be a doozy."

She accepted the glass and sniffed the contents before pretending to gag. "Tequila? No, thank you."

"It's just one." I held up my glass in a toast. "To the biggest flame you've ever conjured."

"And the grease fire that almost burned the house down." She clinked her glass to mine and dumped the contents into the sink.

The back of my throat heated with my slow exhale. That was the last of Mom's potion. I'd have to mix a new batch and find some other way to get Ash to ingest it, and I didn't have time for that.

I tossed back my shot and shuddered as the warm, sharp liquid opened my sinuses. It was fine. Mom had cast the spell on her the day before she and Dad summoned their demon. Ash would be good for another month, and I would be home well before then.

She ducked into the library and came back with a thick, red book. "Don't look at me like that. I wasn't about to let you do two shots and drive away to Hecate knows where. Come sit. I need to look over the protection sigil to make sure I get it right."

I sat in a chair and laid my arm on the table. Ash's eyes darted back and forth as she absorbed the information on the page. My little sister was the smartest person I knew and the most skilled spell-caster I had ever encountered. If she had more self-confidence, she could be the most powerful witch in our coven, even with her fire magic bound. I told her that constantly, but she refused to believe it.

"Got it." She laid the open book next to my arm. "I'll keep it here for reference, though, just in case."

"Dad would be proud to see how well you've done without him to guide you." I laid my hand on hers. "He *will* be proud when I bring him home."

"It's been five months. What makes you so sure they're still alive?" She dipped the needle into the ink and turned on the machine.

I wasn't. Not in the slightest. Even with the veil as thin as it was in Salem, we rarely dealt with demons. And light witches never summoned them...until now.

I had followed our parents into the clearing when they'd taken the grimoire to the demon they'd conjured. I'd hidden behind a tree to witness the trade that was supposed to have happened.

The grimoire and their souls in exchange for a meeting with one of the demons who had cursed us.

But demons were the vilest, most untrustworthy creatures on either side of the veil. If I found the one who tricked our parents, I would come home with his head on a stake. And the three who helped Isabel curse us? As soon as they undid the horror they'd committed on my bloodline, I would send them straight back to the dark prison where they could rot for all of eternity.

"I just am," I finally said.

"That's about as convincing as a vampire saying he's gone vegan." Ash pressed the needle against my skin, the sharp pain jerking me from my thoughts.

"I was there when they were taken, remember?" I winced as she dragged the needle down my arm and looped it upward toward the bend in my elbow. "If the people who took them had wanted them dead, they'd have killed them on the spot."

Ash finished the speed sigil and rested her hand on the table. "I'm not a little kid anymore. If you're making all this up to spare my feelings, don't."

"I'm not making it up. I swear I was there. They were alive when they were taken." Whether or not they still were was debatable. I had no idea what happened to a witch when they crossed the veil, but demons could come to our side unscathed. Logic said it worked both ways.

"Where are you going?" She drew the strength sigil on the other side of my forearm quickly. It was one she'd mastered years ago.

"The less you and Ember know, the better."

"This is utter bullshit, you know? They're our parents too." She tapped my shoulder, and I turned, giving her access to my upper arm.

"I know, but as High Priestess I have to—"

"Maintain certain secrets. I get it." She dipped the needle into the ink and began the protection sigil. "It's still bullshit."

"I'll be back before you know it."

"You better be." She finished the protection and resistance to venom sigils and took a lighter from her pocket.

"I'll activate them later." I tugged my sleeve down and rose to my feet. With my vim still recovering from the mega-cloaking spell I'd just performed, it would draw out all the protection Ash had given me before I made it to my destination.

"Don't forget." She returned it to her pocket. "They don't work unless they're lit."

I grabbed my car keys from my bag. "I won't. Tell Ember I love you both."

She gave me a pointed look. "You can tell her when you get home."

CHAPTER 2
CINDER

"Hiding a skull this far from home is a bit excessive, don't you think?" I mumbled to myself as I rolled my black sedan to a stop behind the church and tightened my grip on the steering wheel.

I supposed Boston was a bit closer to Hingham than Salem was, but still. According to my map app, it would have taken Isabel at least six or seven hours to walk it. And the other hiding spots were even farther away. The woman must've been insane.

Then again, if I'd promised my soul and my first-born child's to a trinity of demon princes, I supposed I'd go to any lengths to avoid paying the price.

The really sad thing was that this whole ordeal... the curse on my bloodline, the promise of souls, the skulls hidden all over...it was all because the man

Isabel loved didn't love her back. How horrible it would be to place all your self-worth into someone else's hands.

I started to feel sorry for her for a minute there, but I snapped right out of that pity party. Plenty of people had been rejected over the eons of our existences, and ninety-nine percent of us didn't resort to cursing an entire bloodline. No, Isabel didn't deserve my sympathy.

Leaning forward, I peered up at the sky and took three deep breaths, centering myself. Wispy clouds stretched across the nearly full moon like silver cotton candy, and an owl hooted from a nearby tree. My stomach growled, protesting the fact that I'd left before Ash could order the pizza.

I was famished, but I'd had to leave before Ember got home from work. Otherwise, she'd have given me the same speech about how I shouldn't be doing this alone, and who was she to lecture me?

If Ember had her way, she'd bust into the church with her sword ablaze, setting off whatever wards or magical traps Isabel had cast centuries ago and getting us all killed in the process.

And Ash...

Her self-esteem was so fragile. Sure, she was level-headed enough to handle the truth if worse came to worst, but hopefully, I could take care of it all so she never had to know. If I'd told them both what I was up to, they'd have insisted on coming with me...and then what?

Someone from our family had to stay in this realm to run the coven if I didn't make it back. As the second oldest, that duty would fall on Ember, and Hecate have mercy, she would hate the job. Hopefully, Ash would be her voice of reason, but if they didn't work together...

No, I couldn't think like that. I had to get the skull, summon the demon, go to Hell, find our parents, and come home. In and out. Quick as lightning. Easy-peasy. *Sure, Cinder. Keep telling yourself that.*

With one more deep, centering breath, I shut off the engine and climbed out of the car. The owl took flight, its wings rustling in the quiet night as I crept toward the church, a two-story wooden structure, beige, with a steeple. A waist-high black fence surrounded the yard, and the gate creaked when I opened it, the sound reminiscent of a nineteen-eighties horror flick.

I half-expected to see rotting zombie hands jut from the earth in front of me, but the grounds remained silent. A single incandescent light bulb burning above the back door cast a warm glow around the entrance, contrasting with the silvery sheen from the moon. A set of four wooden steps led up to the doorway, and a dark brown cellar door lay to the right of it.

Stilling, I closed my eyes and focused inward, searching for the bond I had created with Discord.

Yeah, I know. I know. The only interaction a light witch should have with a demon was to vanquish him, but I didn't have much choice in the matter. Isabel's map was rudimentary at best, giving five possible locations for three skulls *if* you could decipher her squiggly lines and smudged ink. And a cartographer I was not.

I'd snapped a photo of it when I was inside the Boston Magic Society's library, but a five-year-old could have drawn a better map. The damn thing was about as useful as a wad of wet toilet paper.

I was all about working smarter, not harder, so I might have copied down a few dark spells while I was there. And yes, *maybe* one of those spells had to do with binding a demon to yourself, and I *might* have used it to find Discord's skull. Big deal. These were desperate times.

Even light witches had to get a little dark sometimes.

Hell, I was planning to summon a demon prince. That in itself could get me exiled, so why not add a little spice to the good-witch-gone-bad concoction I was cooking up? It was better than my little sister going mad and killing us all.

I took a few more steps toward the entrance.

Another deep breath. More focusing inward. "C'mon, Discord. I know you're in there somewhere."

A tingle formed at the base of my sternum, and a low vibration spread upward through my chest, heating me from the inside out. "There you are."

I followed the tug toward the cellar door and hovered my hands above it. No signs of magic pricked at my palms to indicate a ward, so I tapped a knuckle against the wood. When nothing happened, I dared to press my fingertips against the surface, then my palm. I brushed the back of my hand over the latch, half-expecting to get the shock of the century, but again, nothing happened.

"Okay, then." I gripped the latch and pulled the door open.

A rush of power tingled across my skin, covering me in goosebumps from scalp to toes. I pushed forward, slowly, carefully descending the steps as the remnants of a centuries-old spell clung to my body. *Weird.* This was a passive ward. The funk of magic filled the stale, musty room, reeking like a gas station toilet that hadn't been flushed in months. *Stay away,* it seemed to say, though its voice felt hoarse, like it hadn't been used in a very, very long time.

Pausing at the base of the steps, I waited as it dissipated, whatever effects the caster had intended dissolving around me as the spell unraveled.

Interesting. The mundane had probably been in

and out of this cellar door hundreds of times. I highly doubted they'd felt—or smelt—the spell like I did, so it must've been cast as a warning for any witch who might venture inside in search of the skull.

A warning for most, or possibly a beacon for Isabel's descendants. The seventeenth-century equivalent of a blinking neon sign with a big red arrow that said *here lies skull number one.* It didn't matter either way. I'd made it through Isabel's first line of defense, but I had no doubt it would only get harder from here.

Moonlight streaming in from the open door provided the only illumination in the space, so I lit a fireball in my hand to better see my surroundings. Exposed ductwork lined the ceiling, and metal tubing ran down the walls, enclosing the wiring that had been added long after the structure was built in the late sixteen hundreds.

To my right, a staircase leading up to the ground floor stood next to a shelving unit, but the tug in my gut pulled me to the left, toward an empty wall. I ran my hands along it, searching for a seam or other proof that a door had been plastered over, but I couldn't find anything physical to suggest another room lay behind the wall.

Nothing physical, but the intensity with which my bond with the demon insisted I go through meant magic must've concealed the space. I opened the front zipper pocket on my backpack and pulled out a small envelope filled with powder.

Ash normally packed all our travel potions into glass bottles. Some of them were volatile and would eat through paper or melt plastic, so she preferred not to take chances. This spell was simple, though, and it did absolutely nothing until the incantation activated it. I poured a bit of the powder into my hand and returned the rest to my backpack.

"Magic cloak, I now revoke." I blew the potion onto the wall, and the surface wavered as if I were watching it from the other side of a blacktop highway in the middle of the summer. I counted to three, and the centuries-old shroud slipped away, revealing a wooden wall and a waist-high door with a rusted iron padlock.

"You were one strong witch." I crossed my arms, shifting my weight to one leg as I appreciated Isabel's handiwork.

Not only had her cloak lasted over four hundred years, but it changed with the times. Drywall didn't exist when she cast it, so this spell had adjusted the shroud's appearance to blend in with its surroundings throughout the centuries. How much vim must that have taken? I couldn't imagine.

Footsteps sounded from above, bringing my focus back to the present. I could contemplate super-duper complex spellcasting later. Right now, I had a demon prince to summon.

I hovered my hands first over the door and then over the lock, searching for signs of magic, and Hecate on a hellhound, was there plenty of it. A smart witch would cut her losses and leave it the eff alone, but Discord's skull lay on the other side of this door. The tug in my gut grew stronger, threatening to turn me inside out if I didn't get the damn thing open ASAP.

The door at the top of the staircase opened, and a swath of light penetrated the room. "Who's down there?" a deep voice commanded.

Crap. Out of time. I grabbed a dagger from my thigh holster and beat the pommel against the antique lock. Rust rained onto the floor as it busted, and a pulse of sharp, dark magic shot outward, blasting into me. I careened backward, my body slamming into the shelving unit, the air whooshing from my lungs with the impact.

A can of wood lacquer toppled from the shelf, smacking my shoulder before rolling toward the stairs. The man took two steps down and flipped a light switch, bathing the room in an orange glow.

"I have a gun," he said as he took three more slow steps downward.

I highly doubted a priest in Massachusetts was packing heat, but why take chances? I grabbed another envelope of powder and tossed half the contents at him. "Standing tall or on your knees, in the name of the goddess, I force you to freeze."

His eyes widened as his body immobilized. I had a good ten minutes to get the skull and get the hell out before the spell wore off, so I clambered to standing and dusted off my pants. I was lucky the ward only knocked me off my feet and didn't melt my face off. What was I thinking busting it open like that? That was such an Ember move.

Oh, yeah. I'd connected myself to a demon. The need to get to whatever lay beyond the door had activated something primal inside me. I hadn't been thinking when I'd done that.

The tug in my gut pulled me forward, my feet moving long before they received the signal from my brain. No use fighting it now.

I did take a moment to check for a second layer of wards before I yanked the door open. It seemed the single blast was all Isabel had had the strength to cast after the mega-shroud she'd put on the wall. Or maybe she was counting on what awaited me inside the tunnel to do the heavy lifting.

A deep whine emanated from the darkness, and as I crouched to enter the passageway, the sound turned into a growl. I lit a fireball in my palm, illuminating the dirt walls around me and signaling my location to the snarling beastie guarding the room at the other end of the corridor.

CHAPTER 3
CINDER

You know those hairless Sphinx cats that look like they just crawled out of an alien egg? Imagine that, but five feet long and in dog form. That was the beastie that awaited me.

Its yellow eyes glowed in the dim firelight, and ashy skin stretched taut over its bones. It snarled again, saliva dripping from long, pointed teeth. The poor thing must've been starving, but I wasn't about to become dinner for a hellhound.

"Hey, buddy. I just need that box over there, and I'll be on my way." I touched the flame to each of my sigils, activating them before extinguishing it and clutching a dagger in each hand. "I don't want to hurt you."

Normally, my voice was soothing enough to calm

upset animals and humans alike, especially when I laced it with magic. But not this time. The hellhound stomped a massive paw next to the two-foot wooden box at the back of the small room, and dirt rained from the walls around us. It peeled its lips even farther back, showing me the full length of its teeth as it crouched, shifting its weight to its back legs as if it were ready to lunge.

Well, crap. It looked like I would be hurting the beastie after all. I blew out a hard breath. "I refuse to watch movies where the dog dies, yet here I am, about to unalive you. This is so messed up."

The beast sprang, massive cat claws extending from its doggy paws as it soared toward me. I parried, flattening myself against the wall to slide by it.

It snarled and leaped again. At the back of the room, I had nowhere to go but down, so I ducked. The hellhound landed on my back, its razor-sharp claws cutting through my shirt as it snapped at my head.

Ash's protection sigil did its thing, thankfully, and though the back of my shirt probably looked like jagged ribbons, the hellhound's claws and teeth didn't penetrate my skin. I grunted and threw the beastie off me, slamming it into the wall before grabbing the box o' skull and darting away.

Well, I tried to grab the box and run, but the damn thing was rooted to the ground.

The hellhound plowed toward me, headbutting me and knocking me onto my back. It grabbed my forearm in its massive teeth, and though it still couldn't break skin, the strength of its jaws kept it locked onto me like a vise.

I swung my arm, the strength sigil allowing me to slam the one-hundred-plus-pound beastie into the ground, but still it didn't let go. It hopped to its feet, digging its paws into the dirt and yanking me away from the box.

"I know you're just doing your job, but can you lay off? I'm not leaving here without that skull, and I've got six hours of speed, strength, and protection. Do you really want to do this for that long?"

I jerked my arm from its mouth and felt the first rip of flesh. Its longest canine pierced my skin, creating a three-inch gash as I freed myself from the beastie's jaws. *Shit.* The protection sigil was already wearing off. How could a few bites unravel it so quickly?

I didn't have time to ponder it. The beastie lunged again, this time latching onto my other arm. A fang sliced through my strength sigil, weakening the magic Ash had infused and leaving me no other choice but to unalive the dog.

My fingers tightened around my dagger, and I jabbed it between the hellhound's ribs. The beast yelped and released me. I scrambled to my hands and knees, but before I could get my feet beneath me, it chomped onto my calf.

A flash of heat spread up my leg like my blood cells had turned into razor blades. Every nerve in my body fired at once, the electrical shock making me convulse and bite my tongue.

"Son of a banshee." I'd forgotten to activate the resistance to poison sigil.

The razor blade blood cells crawled up to my glutes, making the muscles contract hard enough to crack a macadamia nut between my butt cheeks. I groaned and shot a stream of fire onto the dormant sigil, and it pulsed on my arm, sending a wave of magic toward the bite.

That was how the hellhound had unraveled the protection magic so quickly. It was strong *and* venomous. Fabulous.

I shot another stream of fire at the beastie's eyes. It yelped and let me go. With the speed magic still intact, I grabbed another dagger and jammed it into the hell-hound's neck. Black blood spouted from the wound. It was no doubt a fatal blow, but if I'd learned anything from the horror movies I loved, it was to always double tap.

I yanked both daggers from the beast, and it stumbled, catching itself against the wall. I swung my blade again and pierced its neck, the tip extending into the dirt wall, pinning the dying beast in place.

My stomach lurched, the bond I'd created with Discord pulling me to the box. As I reached for it, the beast groaned and lashed out a clawed paw, striking me in my lower back.

I couldn't tell you what came over me in that moment, but I'd like to blame it on the demon I was about to summon...because I lost all control. Even with its dying breaths, that hellhound stood in the way of me getting to my demon, and that just wouldn't do.

I slammed a second dagger into the beastie's side before grabbing a knife from my holster and pinning the offending paw against the wall. Reason should have told me not to impale the nearly-dead beast with every weapon I'd brought in, but not a single shred of logic remained in my brain at that moment.

I had to get that skull.

The beast exhaled its final breath, and I turned my attention to the wooden box lying on the floor. It was plain and brown, with no markings or sigils to indicate what lay inside. A pair of hinges lined one side of the lid, but there was no lock or latch keeping it closed.

I laid my hand atop it, searching for signs of magic, but all I felt was a low vibration that begged...no, commanded...me to open it.

So I did.

Inside lay the skull, though it looked nothing like I'd expected. Discord was a demon, so I'd assumed the skull would have horns or tusks or sharp, pointy teeth. Instead, it looked human. Absolutely mundane.

Had I been wrong? Was it possible I'd bound myself to a trickster, and he'd led me to a trap? Dropped me into a hellhound's lair to feed the beast?

My stomach lurched again, the pull demanding I pick it up. The moment my skin touched bone, the vibration seeped into me, making my entire body hum. I jerked my hand away, and the sensation dissipated.

"It's really you, isn't it?" I tilted my head, studying the skull. "Is this a shroud, or do you really look like a human?"

I reached into the box, slipping my hands beneath the jaw and lifting the skull. The vibration penetrated my skin, rolling up my arms and settling in my chest, taking root at the base of my sternum where I'd felt the tug since I'd created the bond.

"I guess we're about to find out, aren't we?" I crouched and duck-walked through the tunnel, rising to my full height as I returned to the church basement.

The preacher, still frozen on the stairs, sucked in a breath. "How?" He squeezed his eyes shut and opened them wide, the only movement the spell allowed. "You passed through the wall."

I scrunched my brow and looked from the tunnel to the preacher. "You don't see the door there?"

He cut his gaze to the wall before looking at me, bewildered. "What door?"

"Interesting." Isabel's cloaking spell was even stronger than I'd thought. It appeared the mundane still couldn't see through it.

I turned toward the exit, and my head spun. "Whoa."

"Are you a ghost?" the preacher asked.

I rested my hand on the shelf to steady myself and cradled Discord's skull in the crook of my left arm. Blood dripped from the three-inch hellhound gash, and though the resistance to venom sigil had done its job, as the adrenaline left my system, I felt every bite the beast had made. *Ouch.*

I cleared my throat. "Yes, I'm a ghost. You'll be stuck there for another five minutes or so, and then you won't remember any of this. Have a nice night."

I limped up the stairs, my injured leg screaming at me with each step, and made my way to the car. My left arm stung like ants were gnawing at the wound, so I set the skull on the hood of my car and grabbed my bag to find a healing salve.

My wounds weren't terribly deep, thanks to the protection sigil, so I rinsed them with a bottle of water and smeared on the salve. The bleeding stopped instantly.

I'd gotten a little blood on Discord's skull, so I poured water over it and was about to set it in the passenger seat next to my bag when the ant bite sensation returned to my arm at triple strength.

"Ow." I ran my finger through the salve, spreading it around on the sting, but it didn't help. The cut mended itself before my eyes, which was absolutely nuts. Our healer, Patrice, was good, but not that good. The type of salve she gave us to carry around wasn't nearly as potent as something made fresh and specific to the wound.

I checked my right arm, and while the bleeding had stopped, the wounds from the hellhound's teeth remained red and angry.

The sensation of a few hundred insects biting my left arm turned into one giant fire ant chomping all the way to my bone. I grunted and was about to smear on the rest of the salve when a series of deep red lines spiraled out from the center of my forearm. At first, it looked like my capillaries were protesting the venom, but as they began to take shape, my stomach dropped so hard, it could have taken my bladder, my intestines, and everything else beneath it right out through my hoo-ha.

I clenched my pelvic floor muscles and ground my teeth until sharp pain shot from my temple to the middle of my cranium. My eyes blinked rapidly of their own accord before I squeezed them shut and opened them one at a time.

Damnit, they didn't deceive me.

Smack in the middle of my forearm, right where the skull had touched my wound, lay a three-inch-long sigil that my sister did *not* design. Ash would never even doodle a demonic mark onto a napkin, much less tattoo one onto somebody's skin.

Yet, there it was. Discord's sigil on my arm.

I rubbed it with my thumb, hoping to wipe it away, but it felt as much a part of my skin as the freckles the sun brought out in the summer. "What the hell?"

I grabbed another bottle of water and poured it over the symbol before using the hem of my shirt to wipe it dry. The sigil pulsed a deeper red.

Eff me. This was not good. The little binding spell I'd cast to join me to Discord wasn't supposed to be permanent. It shouldn't have lasted more than forty-eight hours, and my time was almost up. Of course there was a way to make it stronger, more permanent. It was dark magic, after all, but I hadn't done that. I'd used the simple, temporary, beginner version of the spell. His sigil on my arm meant...

I whirled toward the skull sitting on my hood and froze. "Oh no."

I ripped off what was left of my shirt, doused it with water, and rubbed it on the blood stain. "Oh, shit."

My heart joined my stomach, dropping below my navel, and I swallowed hard as I tossed my shirt into the car and fumbled blindly through my bag for the spare I'd packed, my gaze never straying from Discord's skull.

I pulled the garment over my head and cradled the skull in my hands, lifting it into the moonlight to see it better. On the left side, right above the temple, lay a blueish design that wasn't there before.

A triangle situated in the center of a triquetra, a trinity knot. The symbol for an elemental fire witch.

For *me*.

Holy Hecate in heels. "Blood magic."

I'd made the bind permanent. I, the acting High Priestess of the Salem coven—a coven of *light* witches—had pledged myself to a demon. Permanently.

Maybe.

Truthfully, I didn't know exactly what this meant. The golem guarding the dark witch library hadn't given me enough time to truly research the spell, but I was sure as shit certain having his mark on my body meant something bad.

I closed my eyes and took two deep breaths before opening them and staring into the empty sockets of the demon whom I'd... What exactly had I done?

Had I pledged myself to be his servant? His consort? His bride? I shuddered at the thought.

Maybe it was the opposite. He bore my mark too, so maybe he was mine to command. That sounded like something a dark witch would do. She'd bind herself to a demon so she could control him. She wouldn't choose to be his minion, right?

Ugh! All I knew was that I had accidentally practiced blood magic. This was *so* not like me. With the weight of the entire coven resting on my shoulders, I couldn't afford the luxury of making mistakes...especially ones like this. I never could.

Being High Priestess is a solitary job, my mom always said. *You must be capable of doing it all on your own, and there is no room for errors.*

Well, shit.

"What's done is done. We'll find out soon enough." I climbed into the car and set the skull on my passenger seat before strapping a pair of daggers to my thighs.

Maybe this was a good thing. I was planning to travel to Hell and back, so maybe having a demon prince in my back pocket would come in handy. Or maybe it would be the death of me. Who knew?

Mine was the only mark on his skull, so whatever bond I had accidentally created, he didn't share with anyone else. I could use it to my advantage...as soon as I figured out what *it* was.

I buckled my seatbelt and headed back to Salem. I would summon Discord in the sacred clearing where my parents had summoned the trickster. The veil would still be thinner there, and it was far enough away from home that no one would notice if it formed a little rift.

After leaving my car in a lot half a mile out, I slipped the skull into my bag and hiked the rest of the way. I wanted to run. My leg muscles tightened, begging me to sprint, but I refrained. I walked with long strides and entered the forest, my pulse thrumming as I set down my bag and retrieved everything I needed to summon the Prince of Hell.

CHAPTER 4
DISCORD

When the witch first cast her rudimentary spell, attempting to bind herself to me, I laughed. The magic was weak, but the audacity of the woman intrigued me. The fact someone with such limited skill thought she could not only find me, but summon me, stirred in me the first emotion I had felt in centuries. Possibly millennia.

I had been imprisoned for Lucifer knew how long, denied the use of my senses. Without a corporeal form, my concept of time deceived me. Shadow and darkness, once old friends, had become my wardens, taking pleasure in my mind's demise.

In the beginning, I had stewed in rage, my anger at Isabel, the insolent witch who had tricked me, gnawing at my soul, devouring my essence until nothing but this emotionless shell of a former demon remained.

I had failed my brothers. Failed Hecate and my creator. I barely existed anymore, and I wished with every thread of my being that I would slip away into the nothingness. That I would cease to be.

Then I sensed it. I would like to call it first a tingle and then a pinch, but I had no physical or spiritual form to feel such sensations. So, how could it be?

My consciousness had awakened when the spell took hold, the sensation of my eyes opening, of my lungs drawing a deep breath though I possessed neither in this form, reminding me that I did indeed exist. As the tether formed, no stronger than a single strand of hair, a hint of the witch's essence whispered across the thread. A tiny spark, reminiscent of the fury I felt for Isabel, flared in my being, but it suffocated beneath the weight of my apathy as quickly as it had formed.

This witch was not the one who had vanquished me. The bond she created indicated weak magical ability, mediocre at best. Isabel possessed the power to summon my brothers and myself on her own. Now that she had stolen Hecate's amulet, her strength and that of her descendants would be unmatched.

This witch was neither a descendant nor did she possess the amulet. It wouldn't be the first time someone with limited power attempted to harness mine, but it would be this woman's last.

If the bond she created between us was a true indication of her minimal ability, the vim it would require for her to attempt the feat of summoning me would drain her completely. She would die in the process. Any witch versed in demonology should understand the tax of evoking a Prince of Hell.

Perhaps she knew not of my power, of my rank. Or perhaps she, too, wished to end her existence. The reason mattered not. The conclusion would remain the same. She would die, vim depleted, and I would remain floating in this sensory-deprived state for the rest of eternity.

I should appreciate the entertainment while she made it available. A bonding spell like this would last two days at most, so I...

What in Lucifer's name?

The pinch of the elementary bonding spell turned into a clench. The tether strengthened into steel, wrapping around my essence, penetrating my soul. A stabbing sensation pierced the left side of my imaginary skull, and the sensation of my entire body seizing rocked me to my very core.

That was the binding spell of a worthy witch. An elemental fire witch.

Hours passed, or it could have been minutes or days. Time was irrelevant. Her intent to set me free, however, was overpowering. I felt it through the bond she had created. Her strength, her determination, her sense of urgency... I felt it all, and it was enthralling.

A vibration formed at the base of my would-be head, spreading downward and taking root in my chest. The tether between us tightened, coaxing me toward the barrier of my dark prison, toward the veil.

The prison fought back, shackling my essence with tendrils of despair, but the bond the witch had created between us was stronger than any magic I had ever felt. Her essence called to me, demanding I appear before her. It was a call I could not ignore, not even if I tried.

Her magic, her command, unraveled the prison around me. My shackles dissolved with her intent, and the veil, normally impenetrable for a creature of my level, dissipated into a thin fog, allowing me unhindered passage.

In the form of dark green smoke, I poured through the opening, my essence billowing into the summoning circle the witch had created for me. My skull lay in the center, atop a sheet of parchment bearing my sigil, and my fluid form spiraled around it, my senses returning with overwhelming force, the realm and everything in it coming into sharp focus.

The witch's mark, a triangle inside a triquetra, marred my bone, binding me to her, rendering me incapable of causing her harm in this realm. A clever woman, indeed.

My essence gathered around my skull, the bone absorbing my being as it lifted from the ground. The page bearing my mark sparked flames, burning to ashes in seconds as my body finally took form.

I gasped at the sensation of the cool grass beneath my feet, and I dug my taloned toes into the earth, rooting myself, lest the prison attempt to suck me back through the veil. I fisted my hands and then splayed my fingers, cat-like claws extending from my fingertips before retracting inside them.

I tilted my head, turning it from side to side, my vertebrae cracking into place as I straightened my spine and inhaled my first breath in centuries. The scents of pine, salt, and earth greeted my senses, and I turned around to face the powerful witch who had freed me.

Her beauty slammed into me like a hammer to my chest, taking the breath from my lungs and stilling my newly beating heart. Long hair in a shade of rose I had never seen hung in loose waves down to her waist. Her pink lips formed a perfect bow, and her dark honey eyes seemed to penetrate to my soul.

Her style of clothing indicated centuries had passed since I'd last occupied this realm, her shirt and pants clinging to her body, revealing feminine curves and ample hips. Her skin appeared soft and smooth, and my gaze snapped to her left arm, where my mark glowed red, pulsing in response to my breaths.

Her mark on me. Mine on her. A dangerous bond, indeed.

She raked her gaze down my form and rested a hand on her hip before looking into my eyes. "Hello, Discord."

I arched a brow but said nothing in return as I opened my senses, allowing the energy of both the realm and the witch to wash over me.

"Can you not speak?" She closed the thick book she held and slipped it into a bag with two straps. "I believe a thank you is in order."

I tilted my head, studying her. Strength and power emanated from her aura, but the darkness I expected to find in her soul did not exist. Why, then, did she summon a Prince of Hell and use blood magic to bind us?

"A light witch with questionable morals. You know not what you've done." I stepped toward her but met the wall of a containment spell, which stopped me short.

She crossed her arms. "I know exactly what I've done, what I'm doing, and what you're going to do for me."

I pressed my palm against the magical wall and chuckled. She was new at the dark arts. I could break through in seconds. "My mark on your arm means you belong to me," I lied.

She swung the bag over her shoulder. "Mine on your skull means you belong to me."

"To what end?" I extended my claws and drummed them against the invisible wall. It shimmered with each tap.

She swallowed hard, the first indication of her wariness. "I freed you from your prison. You owe me a favor."

"What gave you that idea?" I laid my other hand against the wall and drummed both sets of claws against it, gently weakening the magic bit by bit.

She flinched, attempting to hide her reaction by straightening her spine. "That's how demons work. I did something for you, so you have to do something for me."

"You want to make a deal, but..." *Tap, tap, tap.* The magic grew thinner. "I am a Prince of Hell. I do no one's bidding."

She laced her other arm through the bag's strap, situating it on her back. "I won't let you out of the circle unless you do, so you might want to change your tune."

"You mean this circle?" I jabbed my claws into the wall and tore it open, the magic unraveling around me as I kicked her ring of salt and prowled toward her.

She gasped, her eyes widening, and she backpedaled into a tree.

"Here is your deal." I wrapped my fingers around her neck and squeezed, pressing her harder against the trunk. "You have bound me to yourself, so I will not kill you. But the last thing I need is a wretched witch following me around. Leave me alone, and I will not make your life a hell on earth."

"No deal," she wheezed, her pulse sprinting beneath my grasp, betraying her fear.

I growled and released her throat, taking her by the shoulders and shaking her. "You know not what I can do."

"I'll send you back to your prison if you don't help me." Her mouth tightened, a tendon in her neck flaring as she ground her teeth.

"Go ahead and try."

"You don't know what I'm capable of." She bent an elbow, showing me the fireball in her hand.

"I was born in the depths of Hell itself. Are you so naïve to believe witch fire can harm me?"

Her nostrils flared, and she slammed the flames against my side in a feeble attempt to cause harm. Perhaps she was so naïve.

The idea intrigued me, or maybe it was the fact this was the first interaction I'd had with another being in centuries. Either way, I *felt* something.

Intrigue, annoyance, and yes, a bit of superiority, which was my right, but underlying it all, I felt the primal, feral need to plant my mouth on hers and make her mine.

Damn the witch and her infernal blood magic.

If she had not bound us together, I would snap her neck and be done with her. Perhaps, when she agreed to revoke her spell, I would. "We must dissolve this connection. Release ourselves from this bond."

"No." Her nostrils flared again, a look of determination tightening her eyes. "I released you from prison. You owe me."

"Hmm." I admired her tenacity. Her fearlessness now that she had recovered from her initial shock. "What is it you desire?"

She inclined her chin. "I want you to give me safe passage to Hell, help me find my parents, and send us back home."

I allowed my gaze to flow over her face, taking in her delicate features and plump, pink lips. "That's three wishes. I am no djinn."

"Then just take me there. I'll do the rest."

I laughed dryly and released her. "No."

"Why not? It's a fair trade."

"No, it is not." I turned and strode toward the trees.

"Hey!" She followed. "Don't walk away when I'm

talking to you." Magic infused each word she spoke. I could feel it caressing my skin, attempting to seep into my mind. She possessed the power of persuasion, the ability to speak with enough finesse and a subtle charm to convince a lesser demon the tarpits were a prime vacation spot.

But I was a Prince of Hell. Her silver tongue had no influence over me. Blood magic, on the other hand...

I stopped and closed my eyes, the magical bond between us making me unable to leave her alone. "I will not take you to Hell."

"Why not?" She circled around to stand in front of me.

"Because I would have to go with you, and it is a place to which I cannot yet return." Not without Hecate's amulet and my brothers' skulls.

"Why can't you?"

"Because I would face the wrath of both Lucifer and Hecate, and that would be a fate worse than the darkest prison imaginable." If I returned empty-handed, Lucifer would fillet me alive, torture me for eons before shredding my soul into oblivion. Hecate would not be so kind.

She pursed her lips, her eyes calculating. "These marks..." She ran her finger over the sigil on her arm, and the sensation of warm velvet sliding over my skin made my entire body shudder with her touch.

"What about them?" I said through clenched teeth, trying not to reveal the effect it had on me.

"What exactly do they mean?"

I let out a slow breath. "They mean we're connected. As long as we bear them, we are one."

"One how?" She slid her hands down her hips, cocking her head.

"The tether. Do you not feel it?"

"I feel something, but I don't know what it is. Tell me." She inched closer.

I growled low in my throat, loath to say it aloud. "Our souls are bound. Over time, if you refuse to remove the bond, it will be difficult to tell where yours ends and mine begins."

She grimaced. "I'm not sure I like the sound of that."

"Neither do I, which is why we must remove it now."

She drummed her fingers on her thighs and narrowed her eyes. "Take me to Hell, and I'll do it."

"I will not."

She huffed and then shrugged. "Okay then. If you're not going to help me, I'll have to vanquish you."

"Our souls are bound. If you vanquish me, you will die." I stepped around her, continuing my trek toward the trees. I grew weary of her already, and I needed time alone to think.

If I could find Hecate's amulet, if it still existed, perhaps it would be enough to save me from the goddess's wrath. Once I obtained it, I would search for my brothers' skulls. With the amulet's power, I could summon them into this realm, and we could collect our price from Isabel's descendants.

Only then could I return to Hell and reclaim my position in Lucifer's court.

"A Holland witch can't be responsible for unleashing a demon on Salem," she called from behind me, stopping me mid-stride.

"You are a Holland witch?" Unmerciful Lucifer, how could it be? "The curse..."

"Hasn't come to fruition." She clutched her hands behind her back and strolled around to face me once again. "You've been in prison for four hundred years, and the whole reason Isabel summoned you hasn't even happened. I and every High Priestess before me have made certain your abhorrent act would never become reality."

My jaw slackened, but I managed to keep my mouth closed. My eyes, however, couldn't hide the fury building inside me. They heated, the green in my irises undulating like molten hellfire. The void of apathy, the nothingness that had once hollowed my being, now filled with disgust and rage.

I had to get away from this woman before I did something I could not undo. I stepped to the right and marched forward, slamming my shoulder against hers as I passed.

A normal person would be terrified in a Prince of Hell's presence. I'd broken her containment circle and come inches from strangling her, but instead of cowering as she should, the witch had the audacity to grab my arm.

"Pisses you off, doesn't it?" she asked.

I spun to face her and ground my teeth, glaring first at her hand on my biceps and then into her eyes. "You have no idea the restraint it is taking for me not to tear your head from your neck. I suggest you let me go."

She loosened her grip but kept her palm pressed firmly against my skin. "What's stopping you?"

I did not appreciate the way her touch, this bond, made me feel. Instead of tearing her limb from limb, I wanted to caress every inch of her infuriating form. "If I kill you, I will be vanquished too. I have things to do in this realm before I can return."

"Mm-hmm." She stepped closer, her mesmerizing gaze locked on me. She lacked the physical strength to hold me in place, but something about her eyes... "And if I die, this binding spell I cast means I go where you go, right?"

I curled my hands into fists. "Unfortunately, that is correct. As long as the bond is intact, if you die, you will go to Hell with me."

"Good. Because that's exactly where I want to go." She moved with a speed only masterful magic could provide. I barely had time to blink before she raised her arm and plunged a silver dagger deep into my heart.

CHAPTER 5
CINDER

Darkness closed in around me. Intense heat, hotter and more putrid than anything I'd ever felt, blasted into my face as if I'd flung open an industrial-sized oven filled with burning, rotten eggs. The sulfurous stench made my stomach lurch. My body seized, the pain of every injury, every cut, bruise, and skinned knee I'd ever acquired in my life flaring to life as if they'd all happened at once.

Holy hellfire and hotdogs. What had I just done?

I dropped to my knees and dragged in a breath. The air felt like thirty-grit sandpaper scraping my lungs. A coughing fit racked my body, and I leaned forward, resting my hands on the rocky ground and preparing to be turned inside-out. My eyes watered and bulged, and snot poured from my nose, the mucus hanging like a gooey icicle as it stretched toward the ground.

Disgusting, I know, but it was the least of my worries.

"What in Hecate's name?" I rasped.

"Silence." Discord slammed a meaty hand over my mouth and kneeled beside me. "Do not invoke the goddess in this realm unless you are prepared to deal with her in the flesh."

I huffed through my nose, breaking the snot chain before sitting upright and wiping beneath my eyes. Discord removed his hand and rubbed it on his thigh, glaring daggers at me as if looks could actually kill.

From him, maybe they could.

I swallowed, my throat so dry and raw that it stuck together and peeled back apart. My tongue felt like a wad of cotton, and my head throbbed like nobody's business. "Why does everything hurt?"

"Welcome to Hell. You'll get used to it. Eventually." He laughed dryly. "Unless, of course, Lucifer discovers you here. In that case, you will suffer for all eternity. Good luck on your journey."

He rose and strode away. I scrambled to my feet and followed, my muscles screaming with each step. How could I ever get used to this? "Wait. You still owe me a favor."

"I owe you nothing." He quickened his pace, heading toward an opening in a rocky wall.

We'd ended up in some sort of massive cave, the ruins of what looked like an ancient temple crumbling to my right. A full Grecian column lay on its side at the foot of an obsidian staircase, the others standing at only half their original heights, their remains lying in pieces around them. A stream of lava flowed up ahead, steaming and curving this way and that as it meandered by, disappearing beneath an arch in the wall.

"I freed you from your prison." I jogged behind him, keeping my gaze trained on his muscular back. "You have to find my parents."

He continued his pace, not bothering to turn around. "Even if I did owe you a favor, I brought you to Hell. My debt would be paid."

"Technically, I brought you." My foot slipped on the uneven ground, and my ankle twisted, searing, sharp pain shooting through my entire foot and making me yelp. *Son of a bitch!* Why was every little ache amplified in this place?

He stopped and whirled toward me, his gaze locking on my injured ankle. His mask of fury slipped for half a nanosecond, his expression morphing to concern...or maybe it was pity. Either way, he recovered quickly and returned to glaring lasers.

"You are correct, *witch*. You vanquished me. You forfeited any debt I owed the moment your dagger pierced my heart."

"My name is Cinder." I rotated my ankle, working

out the stiffness. The movement only intensified the pain.

"Your name is meaningless. You have condemned me, used me to weaken the veil, and created instability in both our worlds. Have you any idea the damage you have done?"

"That wasn't my intention." I slipped off my backpack and lowered to the ground, rummaging through it to find my healing salve. I had to get this pain under control so I could bargain with him. So far, my negotiation skills were spaghetti, he the wall. Nothing would stick. "What do you want, then? What can I do?"

"Unravel the binding spell. Remove our marks so I never have to see your face again."

"What's wrong with my face? It's prettier than yours." I slipped off my shoe and sock and spread the balm over my skin. The swelling subsided almost instantly, but that was the last of the enchanted medicine. Any more injuries, and I was on my own.

Discord let out a deep, rumbly growl, and I peered up at him as I pulled on my sock. He stood over seven feet tall, with dark greenish-gray skin and a wide nose. Thick horns grew from the center of his head, sloping downward before curling up like an African buffalo. His eyes glowed a deep green, and taut muscles rippled down his chest and stomach, leading to powerful legs, and...

Did I mention he was naked? Holy mother of magic, was he.

My tongue slipped out to moisten my lips of its own volition. The heat made me do it. I swear the hot and bothered feeling I couldn't seem to shake came from the intensity of the atmosphere and not the naked demon standing before me.

I forced my gaze to his eyes and slipped on my shoe. "If you want the marks gone so badly, why don't you remove them?"

"If I could, we would not be having this conversation." He narrowed his eyes. "You used blood magic to create the bond. Only you can remove it."

"Find my parents and send us home, and I will." I stood, testing my weight on my ankle. It was angry, but the pain was manageable now.

He stomped toward me, and I did my best not to stare at his junk. Hey, it was swinging side to side like a pendulum, begging me to look. Give a girl a break.

"Witches are liars." He grabbed the front of my shirt in his fist.

My pulse took off in a sprint, as it should with a giant creature from Hell threatening me, but his accusation struck a nerve. Against my better judgment, I just had to poke the demonic bear.

"Careful. I only packed one more shirt." I slapped his hand. He didn't let me go, so I inclined my chin. "Light witches aren't liars."

The green in his irises undulated like lava. "You said you'd remove the marks if I brought you to Hell. Here we are, yet you still refuse."

I grabbed his fingers, trying to pry his hand from my shirt. "Again, I brought you. If you would just listen—"

He snarled and released my shirt, gripping me just below my jaw and digging his thumb and finger into the tender muscles beneath my ears. Stars wavered in my vision, the amplified pain threatening to make me pass out, so I did what any reasonable thirty-year-old woman would do in a situation like this.

I grabbed him by the balls and squeezed.

When he didn't yelp or loosen his grip on my neck, I twisted them hard. Then harder.

His jaw tensed with an audible click of his teeth, the tendons in his neck tightening as he relaxed his grip and released me. With the freedom of movement at my disposal, I lowered my shoulder and twisted even harder, digging in with all the strength I had as I tugged a knife from my thigh holster.

"Touch me again and I'll castrate you." I pressed the tip of my blade against the delicate skin of his sack.

He slowly raised both hands. "Understood."

I let him go and took two steps backward, just to be safe. His dick had the nerve to twitch, and a ghost of a grin crossed his lips before he composed himself. The bastard.

"It appears…" He jerked his head to the right, tilting it slightly as if listening to something I couldn't hear. "The sentry are coming for you."

"What sentry?" I scrunched my brow, trying my damnedest to hear whatever he did. "Why are they coming for me?"

"Their job is to keep out those who do not belong." He cut his gaze toward the darkness to his right. "You are not the first person who has attempted a rescue from this realm."

"We need to hide." I grabbed my backpack and tightened my grip on the knife. "Let's go."

"No." He wrenched my arm behind my back and took my knife in one swift movement. Pressing the blade against my throat, he whispered into my ear, "If you ever wish to leave this realm, you will follow my lead."

"Is that a threat?"

"A word of advice."

I struggled against his grip, lighting fire in my palms and letting it lick up my arms to singe him, but he wasn't fazed. Oh, right. Fire didn't burn demons. I'd have to remember that.

I reached backward, grasping for his balls, but he pressed the blade harder against my neck. Searing pain exploded across my throat, and blood rolled down in ribbons. I had no choice but to stop struggling. I was technically dead, so I had no idea what would happen if he truly slit my throat in this realm. Now was not the time to find out.

Three winged demons approached. They were smaller than Discord, standing maybe six and a half feet tall, but they were just as muscled, and they radiated a menace that chilled me to the marrow. All three had long snouts and pointed ears like hellhounds, but they walked on two legs as if they were some kind of cross between a dog and a harpy.

The most disturbing thing about them was their eyes. They held zero intelligence. No apparent thoughts turned the gears in their primitive brains. One look at Discord and you could tell he was smarter than the average bear, that you could converse and reason with him.

These guys? I had a feeling they had the single-mindedness of rabid dogs. Attack, attack, attack.

"You're throwing me to the wolves?" I whispered.

"You deserve worse for the trouble you've caused me." He straightened, tightening his grip and forcing me toward the fiends.

"What took you so long?" As his deep voice echoed through the cave, the sentry demons froze. Their eyes widened, their mouths dropping open as they stared. The one in the middle lowered to one knee, and the others followed suit, bowing their heads.

"Sire," Middle Guy grunted. "You returned."

"And found an intruder upon my entrance. You

have been slacking in my absence." Regalness deepened his voice even more, his accusation sounding more damnation than chide.

The two sidekicks trembled and barked like dogs. One of them looked up at me and growled.

"Forgive," the middle guy said, and he lowered to both knees, leaning forward and resting his forehead on the ground. The other two whimpered and did the same. These guys were scared shitless.

So was I. Finally, a normal reaction to my predicament.

"If you turn me over to these freaks, I will kill you," I whispered, lacing my voice with as much menace as I could.

"I would love to see you try," he replied before raising his voice. "Take her to my personal prison, but do not harm her. Speak of this to no one."

"Sire." The middle guy stood, and his posse followed his lead. "Small bite?"

"If I hear of a single tooth mark, you all will spend eternity in the tarpits. Do you understand?"

"Yes." They nodded in unison, and he shoved me toward them, yanking off my backpack—with all my weapons and supplies—in the process.

The moment Discord released me, I ran for the ruins. If I could find a hidey-hole somewhere, I might have time to figure out a plan. My boots pounded the rocky ground, and I made it to the first dilapidated step when a harpy-hound dropped in front of me. I spun, but another already stood behind me.

Shifting my weight to my left leg, I kicked my right, my foot landing square in the fiend's gut. He grunted, and I dropped to the ground, swinging my leg out again to knock the other guy off his feet. Before I could make impact, he flapped his wings, taking to the sky and hauling me up by my hair.

Pain exploded across my scalp. I flailed my arms and legs, but it was to no avail. Harpy-hounds numbers two and three grabbed my arms, their grips tight enough to bruise.

"Prison, prison," they chanted and lifted me higher.

"Do not inform Lucifer of her presence or mine," Discord said. "She will be my offering when I return to the castle."

"Your offering?" I screeched and struggled against the fiends' grips. "You're dead, demon man."

He lifted his chin, arching a brow like the arrogant prick he was. "I am afraid *you* are the only one who is dead here. Take her."

He flicked his wrist, and the harpy-hounds hauled me away.

CHAPTER 6
DISCORD

"Son of a bitch." I snarled and slammed my fist into the wall, cracking the stone. The skin on my knuckles split, a flash of intense pain shooting up my arm before it healed. I hit it again with my other arm, closing my eyes to focus on the pain, deepening the sensation, reveling in the brief bout of agony.

It had been centuries since I had felt anything, and the physical was easier to process than the tangle of emotions twisting in my chest.

Cinder Holland sat alone in my personal prison, in a room no magic could penetrate, far from Lucifer's cage for damned souls. I had checked on the way to my clandestine residence, peering at her through a shrouded window so she would not be aware of my presence. Satisfied the sentry dogs had performed their duty, I'd slipped into my secret home unnoticed, and here I stood, paralyzed by the complexity of my situation.

Cinder *Holland*.

A growl rumbled in my chest at the thought of who she was. Of what her existence meant. She'd said four centuries had passed since the vile witch Isabel had imprisoned my brothers and me. Four hundred years of solitude, denied of every sense, left with nothing but the thoughts swirling in my mind until even they ceased to exist.

Until I became nothing...and to what end?

Isabel had summoned us, enchanted us, and promised us two souls in exchange for creating a curse on the Holland bloodline. The third daughter of the High Priestess would go mad, using her fire magic to burn Salem to the ground, murdering the entire coven and any mortals who stood in her way.

The High Priestess was with child at the time, and she had borne two daughters already. The curse should have come to fruition the moment the third reached maturity, but Isabel had vanquished us before we could see the end. She had stolen Hecate's amulet and harnessed its power, giving her strength no being in that realm should possess.

I had shown weakness. I had trusted the wicked woman and let down my guard. I never should have told her who created the stone, what it could do. I had doomed us all the moment the information crossed my lips.

I had won the amulet in a bet with Lucifer long ago, and Hecate had been livid then. The goddess could perform feats of resurrection, and she had promised me the most gruesome deaths imaginable, over and over, if I ever lost it.

With the magical stone no longer in my possession, I could only begin to imagine her wrath. I fisted my hands, my jaw clenching at the imagery my brain conjured.

My brothers and I had spent four centuries in the void, and Cinder Holland was the token to remind me of my oversight, of my blunder. And I had erred once again when she summoned me. The blood bond she had created had clouded my judgment. I had once again let down my guard in the presence of a powerful witch, and now I was trapped in Hell while the amulet and my brothers' skulls remained in another realm.

A being of my status could never cross the veil unless summoned or forced across by Lucifer himself. I highly doubted another witch with the power to call upon a Prince of Hell existed on the other side. That kind of strength was a once-in-a-generation phenomenon.

And Cinder...

I should offer her to Lucifer. The soul of an elemental witch was worth its weight in palladium.

The agony they endured while tortured would provide more fuel than ten mundane souls. He could force her to sever our bond. Then I would be free to return to my post by his side. Perhaps I could take a drink from the River Lethe and forget the past four centuries.

"He would never let that happen." I grunted and dropped into a chair. Cinder's soul might buy the King of Hell's forgiveness, but he would never forget my follies. The Princes of Hell were three, and unless I could bring my brothers home, my royal blood meant nothing.

Lucifer might strip me of my crown and allow me to live amongst the mid-level demons, but I would not survive the shame. And I would still have to deal with Hecate's wrath.

I growled and grabbed Cinder's bag. A strange metal contraption with interlocking teeth held the material closed. I had seen Cinder slide the dangling rectangle over it, unlocking the teeth, so I mimicked the movement and the bag opened as if by magic. It seemed I needed to acclimate myself to the current times if I wished to continue my existence.

Spreading the bag open, I turned it over and dumped the contents onto the floor. Several unlabeled bottles clattered on the stone before a mass of fabric fell on top of them. An envelope lay next to the heap, and I picked it up, finding a fine powder inside. I set it on the table, careful not to touch the contents lest whatever spell the granules contained affect me.

I sorted through the rest of the contents, finding a grimoire, a pair of black pants with tears at the knees, two shirts...one of which had been shredded to ribbons...and a piece of pink fabric with a small metal clasp and two padded, bowl-shaped pouches. Perhaps it was some sort of weapon, like a sling.

The final article was a small piece of pink satin with lace trim. I could not fathom her need for a garment so small, so I shoved everything back inside and rose to my feet. A trip to the seer was in order, but first, I had to mask my identity. If Lucifer or Hecate learned of my presence in Hell, whatever strategy I planned to concoct would never become reality.

In the earthly realm, I could take two forms: my current, true form and that of a man. In Hell, my powers were unhindered, and I could shapeshift as I pleased. I stood in front of the mirror and observed as I transformed. My horns shrank and spiraled as my skin took on the hue of clay. My feet morphed into hooves, and my nose flattened, my cheeks widening and my mouth curving downward as I took on the appearance of a lower mid-level fiend.

My disguise would never fool Lucifer or the goddess, but any passing stranger would be none the wiser. The oracle might see through my cloak, but that was a chance I would have to take. Satisfied with my appearance, I took Cinder's grimoire, ventured from my home, and started down the path to the seer's abode.

The half-demon, half-witch resided in a cave on the outskirts of a town. I made a wide berth around the main square, though the scents of smoked hellcat and stale beer beckoned me to join the minions. There would be time for food and drink later. If I attempted to converse now, my outdated cadence and ignorance of the recent centuries would surely give me away.

A curtain of strung bones hung at the entrance to the woman's home, and I moved them aside to enter. "Seer, are you here? I have an offering and a request."

"Enter," she called from deep inside, her voice rumbly like a demon, with a layer of smoothness atop the gravel to indicate her dual nature.

The antechamber had a domed ceiling, and white crystals embedded in the walls glowed softly next to red demonic runes. I passed through another curtain of bones to find the woman tending to a small cauldron inside a hearth. Tall and slender, she wore a shimmering black dress that flowed to her ankles. Her feet were bare, and she had adorned her curly blonde hair with dried flowers, sticks, and rodent bones.

She hung an iron spoon on a hook above the hearth and turned toward me, half of her mouth drawing into a smile. One side of her face looked like a normal witch, with smooth, fair skin and a deep-set, brown eye. The other half appeared almost melted, the skin a grayish hue, a white sheen clouding the eye.

"Do you require guidance?" she asked.

"Information." I offered the book. "I hope this payment will suffice."

She took it, one brow lifting as she brushed her fingers over the cloth cover. "Where did you get this?"

"From a powerful witch in the earthly realm."

She opened the book, nodding her appreciation as she scanned the pages. "Yes, this will do. Sit." She gestured to a table with two wooden chairs and used a rag to remove the cauldron from the hearth.

I did as she asked, watching her intently as she set the pot in the center of the table and lit two red candles beside it. "What information do you need?"

I chuckled dryly. "Everything that has happened here and in the earthly realm in the last four centuries."

She paused at my request, flicking her gaze to me before turning to a cabinet and plucking two jars of herbs from the shelves. "The history of this realm I can give you. What happened across the veil is shrouded at best. I can see bits and pieces, but to access four centuries' worth of history is a feat only Hecate herself could achieve."

"Show me what you can in relation to Salem, specifically to the Holland coven and their enemies." I leaned forward as she sprinkled the herbs atop the liquid in the cauldron.

She let out a slow breath, regarding me as she sank into the chair. "Sands of time, four centuries deep, reveal yourself to he who seeks." She circled her hand above the cauldron, and her brown eye glazed white to match the other.

"Look," she said as she stared through me, her essence connecting with the energy of the universe.

I gazed into the pot, and the water rippled. My vision blurred, allowing me to see not with my eyes, but with my psyche. In a matter of seconds, I absorbed the last four hundred years in Hell, the changes in language, the magic, a veiled view of the new hierarchy created in my absence. Lucifer had appointed a new trio to fill our ranks, though I could not tell whom he had chosen. It was fascinating and infuriating at the same time.

"I have seen enough of this realm." I leaned back in my chair and shook my head, chasing away the vision.

"Now Salem." She waved her hand above the cauldron again, and I peered into the fragments of time.

I had hoped to find visions of Isabel, of the amulet and my brothers' skulls. Instead, the seer showed me human inventions, automobiles and airplanes, televisions and computers.

"This information is useless." I started to look away, but a swath of shimmering pink hair drew my attention to the vision. Cinder stood facing a man in uniform, her silver tongue no doubt convincing him the magic he'd witnessed wasn't real.

Two women stood behind her, one with purple hair, the other with blue. Such a strange mutation, even for witches. As the uniformed man walked away, Cinder turned to the women, bringing their faces into full focus. Their features were so similar, the shape of their eyes, the curves of their lips. I had no doubt the three were sisters.

I gasped, the realization yanking me from the seer's vision. Cinder had called herself High Priestess. She had two living sisters.

"The curse is coming to fruition. I must go." I rose to my feet, my intention set on returning to the earthly realm. After everything the vile Isabel had put us through, I refused to allow the curse to transpire. I would find her descendants, exact my revenge, and bring my brothers home.

The seer's eye brightened, the iris returning to its natural brown hue. "Be careful, Prince. The gears of fate are moving. May they not crush as they turn."

CHAPTER 7
CINDER

"Frigging harpy-hounds and their dagger claws." I gingerly touched the bruises my wardens had created when they'd shoved me into the cell. I'd tried negotiating with the fiends, explaining my predicament, but I might as well have been talking to a broomstick. All they'd done was grunt and bark the entire way here.

One of them had snapped at me, but the leader had wacked him on the snoot, reminding him of Discord's order not to hurt me. "No bite," he'd said before shoving me into the cell and slamming the door.

I waited until their footsteps receded before grabbing the bars to give them a shake. Big mistake.

A bazillion volts of electricity rocketed through my body, sending me careening backward into a stone wall. My head smacked it with a *thwack*, and my vision wavered as my knees buckled and I sank to the floor.

I squeezed my eyes shut before blinking three times, bringing my prison back into focus. Three stone walls surrounded me, with a gate made of metal bars closing off the rectangle at the front, a stone floor and ceiling adding the finishing touches to my claustrophobic cage.

My palms stung, bright red lines marring my skin where the electricity got me. As a fire witch, I could withstand heat and flames that would cook another witch alive. Needless to say, I wasn't used to getting burned. Not by fire anyway. Electricity, on the other hand, could burn me like a mother... Chemicals too.

I cast my gaze to the ceiling, making sure there wasn't a massive showerhead up there ready to rain acid on me if I tried to escape. The only things occupying space in this cell besides me were a stone slab attached to the wall and a hole in the back corner of the floor that I could only imagine was supposed to be my toilet.

That or it was the passage some hellish animal would crawl through to come eat me in my sleep. *Yikes.*

I scrambled to my feet and peered inside, but I couldn't see a thing. Lighting a fireball in my hand, I held it over the hole, illuminating the top half of the crevice. I still couldn't see the bottom, so I turned my hand over and dropped the flames inside.

A *whoosh* of rancid air shot out of the hole when it reached the bottom, and my fire danced across the surface of a sludgy pool of muck.

Yep, definitely a toilet. *Gross.*

I extinguished the flames, lest I light a ball of methane and create a literal shit storm in my cell, and I tugged my phone from my pocket. No signal, of course. This was Hell, after all.

I set the useless device on the slab and focused my attention on the lock. Fire wouldn't melt it. I knew it wouldn't, but without a spell kit or a lock-picking set, I *had* to give it a shot.

It started as a spark in the core of my being, the magical fire building inside me, gathering in my chest, growing hotter and hotter, until I could no longer contain it. Heat rolled down my arms, blue-tinged flames erupting on my palms before I shot streams of witch fire at the lock.

If I were in a mundane prison, the entire mechanism would have melted. But I was in Hell, so...you guessed it...not a damn thing happened.

I called the fire back and dropped onto the stone slab. I started to hang my head in my hands, but the moment they made contact, the electrical burns screamed at me. *Ugh!* If only I had Patrice's healing salve.

"Think, Cinder. There's got to be a spell that'll bust open this gate without a potion." I racked my brain, sorting through all the charms and incantations I'd memorized over the years. I remembered the spell I'd used to break into the Boston Magic Society's library, but it was a doozy. That spell didn't just open doors, it temporarily neutralized wards and erased all evidence of entry. I'd definitely need a potion for that.

"It has to be something simple. Oh, I know." I rose and stood in front of the bars, holding my hands toward the lock. "Iron bound and sealed so tight, hear my call and yield to might. By flame and force, I break your core. Unlock, unbar, and open the door."

Magic gathered in my chest and flowed down my arms, shooting out my fingertips and entering the lock. I leaned forward, waiting, listening for the tell-tale *thunk* of the mechanism disengaging.

Nothing happened.

"Son of a bitch." I shook my hands and gently pressed my palms together, closing my eyes and trying my best to ignore the pain. "I call on the goddess Hecate. Please hear my prayer and grant me the power to escape this cell."

"You're lucky that cell is enchanted to keep magic from escaping." I recognized Discord's deep, gravelly voice, but I chose to ignore him.

"Hecate, please hear me."

"I warned you not to invoke your goddess in this

realm. You have no idea the extent of her wrath when she finds out what we've done."

I opened my eyes and arched a brow. "What *we've* done? I hope you're not including me in that plurality."

"You are as much a part of the problem as I am." He crossed his meaty arms, his biceps flexing with the move.

"I'm not the one who got bested by a witch. Twice." I mimicked his posture, though my muscles barely protruded beneath my skin.

His brow slammed down, and he stared at me for a few seconds before he spoke. "How did you recognize me?"

I rested my fingertips on my hips, careful to avoid irritating the burns. "I'm the one who summoned you, dingus. How could I not?"

His eyes narrowed. "I'm wearing a shroud. I can change form in this realm."

I shrugged. "You look the same to me."

He flicked his gaze to the sigil on my arm, and it glowed deep red. "Interesting. It seems our bond allows you to see through my disguise."

"Lucky me." I splayed my fingers and dropped my hands to my sides.

"What happened to your arms?" He stepped toward the bars, his eyes tightening even more. "And your hands? I ordered the sentry dogs not to harm you."

"Yeah, well…" I gestured to the bruises before holding up my hands. "And these lovely wounds are courtesy of your electrified bars. If you could turn the pain amplification down a notch or two, that would be fantastic."

He growled, but I couldn't tell if he was mad at the harpy-hounds or at me. "I have no control over the pain you feel. This realm was designed to torture mortal souls. You should not be here."

"And you shouldn't have had your minions lock me up, yet here we are. Let me go so I can find my parents, and I'll get out of your hair." I stepped toward the bars. "Oh, wait. You don't have any."

"You've done nothing but lie since you summoned me. Why should I release you?"

I focused on my inborn gift, lacing my words with persuasive magic and making myself appear confident and in charge. "You know I'm not a threat. All I want is to find my parents and take them home. If you help me, I'll be gone before you know it."

A deep chuckle emanated from his chest. "I can feel the silver-tongue magic you're attempting to use through our bond, but you're wasting your vim. Magic can't escape your cell, and even if it could, I am immune to your wicked power."

I ground my teeth because, dammit, he *was* immune. He'd have brought me to Hell willingly if he wasn't. "First of all, my power is not wicked. I never make anyone do anything they don't want to."

He scoffed. "I'm sure you do exactly that all the time."

"I do not." I reached for the bars, but they zapped my fingertips before I could grab them. "Son of a banshee." I shook my hands and took a step backward so I wouldn't be tempted to do it again.

"What you call my silver tongue is passive magic. It's not mind control, and I'm not taking away anyone's free will. It only affects me, not the person I'm talking to, so if you're feeling something when I do it, it's because of that symbol carved into your skull." I held up my arm. "And because of this."

"Which you *will* remove."

If only I knew how. Other than my bleeding on his skull, I had no idea how I'd formed this intense bond, and I doubted reversing the simple, *temporary* connection spell I'd cast would do it. But I couldn't let him know that. For now, it was best he thought I simply refused.

Refusing put the power in my hands. "Are you sure you want me to do that? I can see through your disguise, thanks to our bond, and you can see through my influence glamour. If I remove the marks, you'll be exposed to my full potential. You'll *want* to help me find my parents. Believe me, I am very persuasive."

"Hmm." He extended a claw and ran it across the

bars, making a *tink, tink, tink* sound. Apparently, the hex on my cell only affected the person inside it.

I blew on my palms, willing the agonizing burn to subside. My attempt only made it worse. I sank onto the stone slab and rested my hands atop my knees, breathing deeply and focusing on my thoughts rather than the pain.

I was useless inside this cell. All I'd seen in this realm so far were the massive cave-like entrance and the inside of these walls. When the harpy-hounds had whisked me away, they'd flown so quickly that my surroundings had blurred. I had no idea where my parents might be, nor how to get out of this realm once I found them.

Discord was my only ticket home. Maybe I should start being nice. "Look, I'm sorry I vanquished you. It's just... My parents are here because a demon tricked them, and I really, really need to take them home."

"Your role as High Priestess began because your mother made a deal and paid the price." He leaned against the wall beside the gate. "Now you've attempted the same and left me no choice but to imprison you."

"No, this is different. I never offered you my soul." I winced at the stabbing burn in my hands and shook them.

"Yet you've bound mine to yours." He inclined his chin. "You're in pain."

"No shit, Sherlock." I stood and paced the width of my cell. "Your hex nearly turned me into a Kentucky fried witch."

His brow furrowed. "I don't understand your references."

"Of course you don't."

"Stand still."

I turned toward him. "Why?"

He inhaled deeply, his gaze locked on his sigil on my arm. The mark glowed again, growing brighter and brighter until a cooling sensation spread through my entire body. My skin tingled, my muscles contracting and then relaxing as his essence washed through me.

"Better?" he asked.

My head spun, and I rested a hand against the wall to steady myself, gasping and jerking it away when I realized what he'd done. "You healed me. How?"

"My power is immense in this realm."

"I bet." I laughed dryly and held my wrist, gazing at my palm. Once red and angry, my skin was now smooth and unmarred. My other hand was normal too. I rotated the ankle I'd rolled earlier, and it moved freely, without a shred of pain. The glow on the sigil subsided, and the cooling sensation dissipated from my body.

I rubbed my hands together and looked at him quizzically. "Why did you help me?"

He opened his mouth to respond but closed it

quickly, his expression morphing into one of confusion. "I didn't like seeing you in pain."

"Why not?"

He huffed a breath through his nose. "I assume the magic connecting us has infused me with empathy toward you."

"Then why won't you let me go?"

He straightened, his chest expanding as he recovered from his moment of uncertainty. "You have no idea the extent of damage—"

"You keep saying that. The extent of damage, the extent of wrath, the extent of my boot up your ass if you don't stop being so cryptic." I crossed my arms, shifting my weight to one leg. "I'll continue to have 'no idea' until you tell me, so why don't you explain it to me like I'm five to be sure I understand. Or do you think I'm too stupid to comprehend the 'extent of everything' I've caused?" I made air quotes and crossed my arms again.

"You must be stupid to voluntarily cross into Hell. Apparently, it's genetic." He mirrored my posture, so I dropped my arms to my sides.

"Fine. Don't tell me anything." I rested a hand on my hip. "Leave me here to rot, and you can deal with all the 'extents' yourself."

His lips twitched. "You have two sisters."

"And?"

"You said the curse that cost me four hundred

years of my existence hadn't come to fruition, that you and every High Priestess before you made certain it never would. Yet a third daughter exists in your realm. You lied."

"I didn't lie. I *am* making sure it doesn't happen. That's why I'm here." I started to reach for the bars but thought better of it. "Wait. How do you know about my sisters?"

"The seer showed me all I missed of this realm while I was imprisoned. She attempted to show me Isabel in yours, but the vision focused onto you and your sisters before it dissipated."

"Then you know it hasn't happened yet. My parents summoned a demon who promised to deliver you to them. That plan didn't work out in their favor, so I did a little breaking and entering and committed a few magical crimes to find you myself, and here we are."

I spread my hands. "You're going to break the curse."

He laughed. "Perhaps I would have complied, had you not vanquished me prematurely."

I shrugged. "My parents are suffering. I had to improvise."

"You—" He froze, his muscles going rigid, a white glaze forming over his eyes. He didn't breathe, didn't so much as twitch a lip as he stood there in what looked like some sort of trance.

"Discord?" I focused on the connection I'd formed with him, searching the invisible tether that should have connected us for a sign of life, but I felt nothing. It was as if someone had plucked his consciousness from his body, leaving only an empty shell.

The tether tightened, the low demon vibration I'd grown accustomed to returning, getting deeper and slower. A snake-like sensation slithered along the invisible cord, making my stomach turn as it approached. The sigil on my arm heated and glowed, and it felt like a metal wall slammed down, stopping the sickening advance.

Discord gasped and blinked, the white film over his eyes dissolving as he locked his gaze on me. "Lucifer has summoned us."

"Us?" My heart dropped. Attending an audience with the devil himself definitely wasn't on my bingo card today...or any day for that matter. "He knows I'm here, and he wants to see me too?"

He nodded. "Indeed. And if you wish for your soul to survive, you will do exactly as I say."

CHAPTER 8
CINDER

"You will do exactly as I say." I crossed my arms and parked my butt on the bench, mocking Discord's last words. The moment he'd uttered them, he'd turned on his heel and strode away, leaving me here to ponder my soul's survival alone.

"If you want me to do as you say, you actually have to say something," I yelled into the abyss.

How dare he glare at me with those dark, moss-green eyes, make such an ominous proclamation, and then just walk away. For all he knew, Satan could have swooped in and had me for breakfast by now. Or would it be dinner? My watch had died when I'd arrived in the underworld, taking my concept of time with it.

I couldn't tell you how long I sat there waiting, but

it was long enough for me to check every nook and crack in the stones around me. The walls had to be three feet thick, the ceiling a solid slab of rock. Unless I wanted to squeeze myself through the hole in the floor and swim through eons' worth of demon doo, I was stuck in this magic-proof box until dear old Discord decided to set me free.

"Well, Cinder. What now?" I exhaled, trying to blow a strand of hair from my face, but it refused to budge. Between battling the hellhound in my realm, summoning a demon prince, and then fighting off harpy-hounds in Hell, my skin had gotten a tad greasy.

I gathered all my hair, pulling it forward, over my right shoulder, and raking my fingers through the tangled strands. I'd need a facial and a deep conditioning treatment by the time this was through.

Footsteps echoed from one end of the hallway, bouncing off the other end until it sounded like they came from all around me. My heart tried to jump into my throat, but I swallowed hard and rose to my feet, instinctively reaching for the dagger that should have been strapped to my leg. I was defenseless inside this magic-proof box, so I dug in deep and poured all my vim into what Discord called my wicked silver tongue.

The power had nothing to do with my tongue, really. It was a sort of inborn glamour, a way for me to make myself appear more confident, capable, and smart. Confidence was the key, and when I spoke, it sounded like I was the authority on whatever topic I discussed. It helped that I was the eldest sister, the first in line to become High Priestess as soon as my mom retired.

I'd been training for leadership my whole life, and this special little power came in handy on the daily. People looked up to me. I had to at least appear like I wouldn't let them down, even when I felt like I would.

I steeled myself, lifting my chin to add to the glamour as Discord stepped into view. "Oh, it's just you." I let out a slow breath.

"Come with me." He extended a claw and twisted it in the lock. The electrified gate that had nearly turned me into chicken-fried witch *thunked* and opened about half a foot.

I nibbled on my bottom lip, contemplating my options. My boots had rubber soles. Rubber didn't conduct electricity, so in theory, I could kick it open and run through without melting off my toenails. But that theory involved the electricity being mundane, and I highly doubted the Prince of Hell relied on human technology to keep his prisoners at bay.

I could attempt to squeeze through the narrow opening, but Mother Nature had blessed me with too much junk in the trunk for that to be feasible. With my luck, I'd nick the bar with a butt cheek and end up with a rump roast to make Sir Mix-a-Lot cry.

Thankfully, my captor didn't give me time to

ponder any more ways to cook myself. He grabbed a bar and pinned me with a warning stare. "I'm going to open the gate. I advise you not to try and escape."

"That's your advice, eh?" I inched toward the threshold, cutting my gaze right and left, calculating my chances. "Afraid I can outrun you?"

"Not at all, but we are currently in the eighth level of Hell. Even if you made it back to the first level, you'd be stuck. No one gets out without Lucifer's blessing, and he's not the most generous man you'll ever meet."

"Orpheus did it." I jutted out my chin.

"And look how it worked out for Eurydice."

"Dante then."

"Virgil, I am not. Come, Lucifer expects us in an hour. We must appear presentable." He swung the gate open, and I did what any smart woman who'd written herself a one-way ticket to Hell would do.

I stepped into the hall, spun in a circle to take in my surroundings, and waited by his side. Listen, I wasn't an idiot. If Lucifer knew I was there and had sent word that he wanted to see me, what chance did I have on my own?

Zip.

I wasn't in the mood to have my soul shredded by the King of Hell, so I'd better play make believe and at least appear like I was worthy of his company. If he wanted to slice my existence into strips and fry me like bacon, he'd have done it already, right?

"This way." Discord grabbed my biceps and dragged me down the hall.

I tried to jerk from his grasp, but his hands were huge, completely encircling my arm, and man, oh man, was he strong. "I can walk on my own."

"I'm sure you can." He tugged me harder, and the atmosphere thickened. Heat and oppressive humidity gathered around me, pressing, squeezing until I thought my eyes would pop from their sockets.

One step forward. Two steps. It felt like I was moving through a gelatin mold until...*pop*. The pressure dissipated, and the darkness around me bled into light. I gasped and pressed a hand to my chest. If I'd had pearls, I would've clutched them.

A city stretched out before me, the towering buildings made of basalt and obsidian glass. A stream of lava flowed down the center of the street, and arched foot bridges connected the two sides at varying intervals. The sky was deep orange, and clouds in twenty shades of red stretched across a golden... I couldn't tell if it was a moon or a sun, but its light cast the city in an eerie glow.

An obsidian palace rose in the distance, blocking my view of the horizon. Black glass reflected the orange light, making it appear to glow, and spiraling turrets jutted upward, extending into the clouds.

I turned around, peering behind me toward the exit, but it wasn't there. "How?"

"My prison is in a secret location. A pocket in the realm that only I and the lead sentry dog can find." He tugged me into the city. "We must get inside before we draw attention."

We strode up the right side of the lava stream and passed a bar where demons and humans alike tossed back brews and shouted drunkenly. Heavy metal music drifted from an open window, and a beastie with yellowish-gray scales lifted a pint in my direction, his smile revealing dozens upon dozens of cylindrical, pointed teeth.

The savory scents of meat and spice drifted from the next storefront, where a woman with brown leathery wings stood at a counter, rolling dough. The sign above the door read Lilithina's Meat Pies.

My stomach growled, and I slowed my stride. "Any chance we can make a pitstop for a pie?"

Discord tugged me along. "Lucifer will provide a feast unlike any you've ever seen. Enjoy it, as it may be our last."

"There you go again with those ominous statements. Will you please tell me what's happening? How does he know we're here? Why does he want to feed us?"

"In here." He dragged me through a doorway and pressed a button on the wall.

"You use elevators in Hell?" My mouth hung open, so I snapped it shut. Aside from the lava stream, the beasties, and everything being black, Hell looked so… normal.

"We're heading to the thirtieth floor. Would you prefer to use the stairs?" He finally loosened his grip, and I tugged from his grasp, rubbing my arm and rotating my shoulder.

"Elevator's good. Is this an apartment building?"

The door slid open, and he stepped inside. "Yes."

I followed. "Do you live here?"

He missed a beat in his reply. "No."

Gravity made me heavy on my feet as the elevator whisked us upward. "Then why are we here? Where do you live? Or…where did you live before you were imprisoned? In that palace?"

He cut me a sideways glance. "You ask too many questions."

I parked my hands on my hips. "If you would tell me what the actual eff is going on, I wouldn't have to. This stoic, man-of-few-words persona might've worked on women in the seventeenth century, but we have agency now. I want answers."

He growled softly and grabbed my hand, pulling me out of the elevator and, once again, dragging me down the hall. Shiny red sigils dotted the black wallpaper, glittering as we passed, and my heels thudded on the black marble floor as we made our way to the door at the end of the hall. He pushed it open and gestured for me to enter, but I held my palms toward him.

"You expect me to walk in first when I have no idea what's inside?" I arched a brow. "I'm not leaving this hallway until you answer my questions."

"As you wish." He crossed the threshold, and the door swung shut behind him.

"Are you kidding me?" I grabbed the knob, but it wouldn't budge. The nerve of that man! "Open the door, Discord."

Silence answered me, so I pounded it with the side of my fist. "Open it right now, or you will regret it."

"Will I?" Amusement tinged his words. "And what, fair witch, will you do if I refuse?"

I opened my mouth to respond, but he had me there, didn't he? I was a light witch in a dark realm, bound to a demon prince, with the ruler of the Underworld expecting me to show up for dinner any minute now. I was screwed.

"If you take me to Lucifer looking like this, he'll probably shred my soul. What do you think will happen to you when he does that?" I moved closer to the door, resting my palm against it and lowering my voice. "With my soul bound to yours, I imagine it would be painful for both of us. We may be on your turf, but I think, right now, you need me as much as I need you."

Five seconds of silence passed before the knob

turned and the door swung open. I stepped through the threshold before either of us could change our minds and found myself inside a demonic penthouse apartment.

Translucent red tiles covered the floor, and the wall to my right had streams of what looked like lava flowing down it, disappearing into a black marble drain beneath. A hellcat-skin rug lay in the center of a recessed living room, and leather couches formed a U shape around it. I didn't dare ask where the leather came from.

A black suit lay across the back of the nearest sofa, and Discord picked it up, draping it over his arm. How he planned to fit his massively muscled body into a human-sized outfit was beyond me.

"She is a pretty one, Discord," a demon purred as she stepped out of a room to my left. "I can see why she was able to disarm you."

I fisted my hands as she slinked toward me. Her forked tongue darted out from plum-colored lips, and her yellow irises constricted, her pupils turning to vertical slits like a cat. Aside from the eyes and tongue, she could've passed as human, with umber skin, long, flowing hair, and a shimmery gold dress that was slit up to her hip.

"She did not…" He blew out a hard breath. "She needs clothes. Something worthy of an audience with Lucifer."

The demon looked me up and down. "If she hadn't already bound herself to you, I'd demand you let me have my way with her as payment."

Discord's nostrils flared. "You owe me, Belira. Don't forget that."

She laughed. "You'll never let me. You could join us...just like old times."

Oh. She was a succubus. I'd let him lure me into the lair of a sex demon, and she was an old flame who wanted a three-way to boot. Fabulous.

His jaw tightened. "Four centuries later, and you still try my patience."

Her tongue flicked out again. "You wouldn't have me any other way. I have just the outfit for a first meeting with our dear king."

She disappeared into the other room and returned with a strappy, red sequined dress and a pair of black platform stilettos.

"I am not wearing that." I gave Discord a pointed look.

His eye twitched, and a series of emotions crossed his face before he shook his head. "As beautiful as she would look in it, I prefer her in something more modest."

I scoffed. "*You* prefer...?"

He cocked his head. "With long sleeves to hide my mark on her arm."

"You're a fool if you think Lucifer won't sense it," Belira said.

"I don't doubt he will, but I prefer not to advertise my folly to the entire court."

She pursed her lips and disappeared into the other room again.

"Did you seriously bring me to your old girlfriend's house?" I whispered.

He shrugged. "You asked me for help. I'm helping."

"I asked you to help me find my parents."

"You have no idea how things work here."

"Because you won't tell me shit!" I whisper-shouted, throwing my hands into the air.

"Here." Belira returned with a shimmery black number, strapless on the right side, a long sleeve on the left.

"That will do." He took the dress and platform heels and laid them on the sofa. "Leave us. And not a word of my...predicament...to anyone."

"Your secret is safe with me." She winked and slithered toward the door. "Bring her by if you both survive. I promise it will be a hell of a time."

I waited for the door to click shut before whirling toward Discord. "What the actual...whoa."

The demon I'd summoned, with his dark green skin and buffalo horns, was gone, and in his place stood a tall, chiseled, completely naked man. "The shower is through that door. Clean yourself, and I will answer your questions."

"Or you could answer them now." I crossed my arms and forced myself to look at his face rather than... the rest of him. He had the same dark, moss-green eyes as before, but that was where the similarities ended. Instead of horns, he had thick brown hair, sheared short on the sides, and a peppering of a five o'clock shadow accentuated his strong, sharp jaw.

He curled his lip and pulled on his pants before gesturing to the door in question. "You reek of hell-hound and sweat."

I fought the urge to sniff my pits and grabbed the dress instead. "Fine. I'll take a shower, but you better be here, ready to talk, when I'm done." I turned on my heel and strode into the bathroom.

CHAPTER 9
DISCORD

Why must women be so infuriating?

I buttoned the dark burgundy shirt Belira had acquired for me and slipped on the jacket. It had scarcely been a day since Cinder freed me from prison, and I had already subjected myself to yet another insolent woman.

Sadly, I had no other choice. To appear in Lucifer's court in demon form would be an insult to our kind. To take Cinder in her present state of disarray would secure us both reservations in the tarpits for the rest of eternity.

The sound of the shower shutting off drew my attention away from the mirror and toward the bathroom. Cinder would be drying herself, preparing to don Belira's dress. Temptation to step inside and take her had my cock hardening for the first time in centuries.

The witch was beautiful. Of that there was no doubt, but I had to remain in control of my desires. Until I discovered where I stood with Lucifer, I had to focus on the issues at stake. Freeing myself from Cinder's blood bond came second only to securing my safety in Hell.

The bathroom door opened, and Cinder stepped out. The dress clung to her curves, emphasizing the roundness of her backside. The single sleeve hid the visible evidence of our bond, and she pulled her damp hair forward, attempting to rake a comb through the tangles.

"All right, Duke of Darkness. Start talking." She clutched her hair halfway down and jerked the comb through the ends. "Why does Lucifer want to see us, and how can I find my parents?"

"One of the sentry dogs must have spread word of our arrival. The fact he had the gall to disobey the authority of a prince does not bode well."

"Is it gall or is he just a moron?" She moved the comb higher in her hair, picking at an unruly knot. "Harpy-hounds aren't the sharpest daggers in the collection, are they?"

"No, they are not." I chuckled and held out my hand. "Allow me?" We'd never make it to the palace at the rate she was working.

She arched a brow, studying me for a moment before placing the comb in my palm and turning toward the mirror. "I don't think demon conditioner is made for mortal hair."

I lifted a lock and worked the comb through the ends. "Most mortals don't come to Hell willingly, nor do their corporeal forms survive the transition."

"We passed a bar full of humans on our way here." She adjusted the top of her dress. "Or maybe not humans. They could've been witches or shifters, I suppose, but they didn't appear to be writhing in torture."

I laid the first lock of untangled hair over her shoulder and moved on to the next. "Trust me. They were demons. Only those of the highest levels can assume a human form, so they flaunt it to show their status."

She watched my reflection intently. "I suppose old Satan will look like a man when we arrive?"

"He will, and I would advise you not to call him by that name."

"Why not?"

"Lucifer has had many names over the eons, but that one was derived from a misinterpretation of the Christian Bible, and it's only used in derogatory ways."

She whistled. "Guess we shouldn't insult the king on our first meeting."

"I'm glad you understand." I continued combing the knots from her hair.

"What about Hades? Is that acceptable?"

"You are about to meet the ruler of the Underworld, arguably the most powerful man in all the realms, and he hasn't been known for his benevolence in thousands of years. Do not assume yourself so familiar with our king as to call him by any name. Speak only when spoken to. Refer to him only as sire or your majesty until he tells you otherwise."

She scoffed. "He's not my king."

"You are in his realm illegally." My pupils constricted, the green of my irises billowing like smoke at her insolence. "Your rash decision to vanquish me has endangered both our souls, and I won't allow you to throw away our chance at making it out intact by running your wicked mouth."

A growl rumbled in my chest as I worked out the last knot. "I should have killed you the moment you summoned me."

She narrowed her eyes. "Yet here you stand, in your ex-girlfriend's apartment, brushing my hair as if we were lovers. Where did you learn how to do that?"

"Isabel." I slammed the comb onto the table beneath the mirror. "We were intimate. I won't make that mistake again."

She grinned and turned toward me. "Are you trying to convince me of that? Or yourself?"

If I were honest, I'd say both, but demons weren't known for their truthfulness. The bare skin on her shoulder appeared smooth, fair, and it beckoned me to caress it. The bitter scent of myrrh shampoo did nothing to mask the sweet vanilla undertones of her pheromones, and the way her dress shimmered with her movement, drawing attention to her curves, had my dick hardening all over again.

I grabbed her left hand and shoved up her sleeve, revealing my mark on her arm. The moment I touched it, my temple tingled, reminding me how strongly we were connected. "Remove the blood bond."

She tugged from my grasp and pulled the sleeve down. "Send my parents and me home, and I will."

"If Lucifer hadn't summoned us, I would have left you in your cell to rot until you agreed."

"Yet here we are." She spread her arms in a presenting motion. "We better not keep Luci waiting."

This woman would be the end of me. I narrowed my eyes and strode to the door, opening it and gesturing for her to exit. "There are fates worse than death...to which Lucifer would be pleased to condemn us both."

"And now we're circling back to my questions. What's going on and why is it happening?" She stepped into the hall and waited as I closed the door. "If what I read is true, you're the most powerful prince around. Everyone should be cowering in your presence, doing exactly what you command. It should be easy for you to demand the release of my parents and send us home."

Was she really so simple-minded? "My brothers and I were Lucifer's most trusted friends. We commanded his army, advised him, and we were his closest confidants."

"I take it 'were' is the key term here?"

I pressed the button to call the elevator and smoothed my jacket's lapel. "Indeed. I have no doubt our imprisonment brought shame to the palace, and the seer showed me the unrest amongst Lucifer's subjects when he lost his top three men. It has taken him centuries to right the balance."

"Who did he replace you with?" The elevator doors slid open, and she stepped inside.

I followed and pressed the button for the ground floor. "I do not know. What happens inside the palace is shielded from prying eyes...now even from mine, it seems."

"Why didn't he set you and your brothers free? Isabel was just a witch, and he's the King of Hell. If he's the most powerful man in all the realms, couldn't he have yanked you out and returned you to your posts?"

The doors opened, and I strode into the lobby,

stopping a few feet from the exit. "Lucifer has never been one to stand between consequence and a fool."

Her boot squeaked on the obsidian floor as she approached. "Don't be so hard on yourself. Isabel was a woman scorned, and I wouldn't wish that kind of wrath on anyone."

"Where are the shoes Belira gave you?" I eyed the ankle-high combat boots she wore.

She lifted her dress and rotated her ankle. "If we're in as much danger as you say we are, I'm not about to face it in platform stilettos. I'd break a leg before we even made it to the palace if I wore those things."

I wanted to argue her footwear could be taken as an insult, but I had a feeling shoes were the least of my worries with her. If only I had thought to purchase a silencing spell from the seer when I was there.

"Come," I said instead and exited the building.

"You said I'm here illegally. What does that mean?" She hurried to catch up and walked by my side.

I glanced at her sideways before focusing on the palace in the distance, a sickening feeling growing stronger in my stomach with each step. "Your soul is unclaimed. You're here neither by Death's hand nor by a demon's bargain. Unclaimed souls find their way to Hell for one of two reasons. Either they wish to resurrect a claimed soul, or they intend to infiltrate and start a war."

"Well, I'm definitely not here to start a war." She eyed the palace in the distance. "What usually happens to unclaimed souls when Lucifer discovers them?"

"If he's feeling merciful, obliteration. Otherwise, an eternity of torture in the deepest circle of Hell."

"Hold up." She stopped and rested her hands on her hips. "So...what? You got me all dressed up as an offering? You're planning to turn me over to save yourself?"

"If it were that simple, I would." I continued walking. "Your blood bond has complicated the matter."

"Because if I get obliterated..." She strode toward me.

"I do too."

"So I'm not unclaimed, then." She jerked up her sleeve. "This means you claimed me. I'm with you, so I'm not illegal."

I stopped and clutched her hand, tugging the sleeve down. Several demons had gathered in the street to watch us pass, and a group crowded around a window in the café to our right. I straightened my spine and turned around to address them.

"As you were. This is none of your concern." I tilted my head slightly, widening my stance when no one moved. The sourness in my stomach rose upward, solidifying in my chest and making my voice rumble. "As you were."

They cut their gazes toward each other, mumbling amongst themselves as if confused. Anger sparked in my gut, the heat rolling outward, consuming me. I refused to tolerate their insolence.

Magic gathered in the core of my being, and my vision sharpened, my demonic form simmering just beneath the surface. If I'd had the time, I'd have torn a few limb from limb for their disobedience. Then, the rest would cower at my feet as they should.

Instead, I focused on their minds, sowing discord into their masses.

"You sorry sack of shedim shit!" A capras demon shoved an incubus before landing a punch on his jaw. "You seduced my wives."

"I'd never touch anything that ugly." The incubus spat blood and barreled into the capras, tackling him.

A goblin snickered, and a chasm demon whirled toward her with malice in her eyes. "Oh, you think it's funny? I bet you thought those rumors you spread about me were funny too."

The crowd's mumbling turned into shouts. They shoved, punched, and kicked, wrestling each other and casting blame for things that never happened.

"What in Hecate's name?" Cinder's lips parted as she took in the disarray.

I sent one last pulse of magic into the crowd before clutching her hand and pulling her toward the palace.

"What was that about?" she asked. "Why did they suddenly turn on each other?"

"Because I made them. The sooner we can get inside, the better. It appears my authority in the realm ceased with my imprisonment. I must regain Lucifer's favor if we wish to survive."

She swallowed hard. "We. You said we because you claimed my soul, right?" She lifted her sleeved arm.

I gave my head a hard shake and spoke through clenched teeth. "Do not flaunt that mark. It doesn't mean I've claimed you."

"What does it mean?"

"It means *you've* claimed *me*. That I was, once again, bested by a witch. My folly forced me to abandon my post for over four centuries, and now you've brought me home empty-handed. My brothers are still imprisoned, and Hecate's..."

"What about Hecate?"

"Walk faster. Lucifer has filleted people for far weaker infractions." I tugged her along, using my power to alter the space between us and the palace, bending the distance so we crossed miles in seconds. When I released my hold, my head spun. My body was no longer accustomed to existing, much less performing such magical feats.

Neither was Cinder's, it seemed. She pitched

forward, expelling the acid from her stomach onto the ground. "What the hell?"

She swayed on her feet and collapsed into my arms, her eyes rolling backward before her face went slack.

CHAPTER 10

CINDER

My head pounded like someone was beating it with a heavy rubber mallet over and over and over. My stomach roiled, and I rolled to my side, dry heaving, which meant I had already expelled whatever food it had contained when I'd arrived in the Underworld. Lovely.

"What the actual eff?" I hoped to Hecate I didn't get anything on my dress. From the way Discord had described Lucifer, I doubted he'd appreciate me wearing my lunch to dinner. Speaking of my demon...

"Discord?" I rasped, my throat dry and rough. I opened my eyes, and shadows encircled my field of vision. Floating pinpricks of light danced around it too, making it hard to focus.

A shadow moved in front of me, and the scraping sound of metal rings on a pole pierced my skull as he shoved the curtains aside. A dust cloud billowed from the fabric, and reddish-orange light spilled into the room, making me squint and cough at the same time. I sat up and clutched my aching head. "Ow."

"Can you stand? Lucifer expected us ten minutes ago." He stood in front of me and offered his hand. I didn't accept it.

"What the hell just happened to me? Why do I feel so sick?" The haze in my vision dissipated, and I took in my surroundings. I sat on some kind of fainting couch made of black wood and midnight blue upholstery. Black slate covered the floor, and red runes and sigils covered the walls.

Discord gestured with his hand again, silently suggesting I take it. "I used demon magic to bend the space between the town and the palace to get us here faster. Apparently, your body can't handle that kind of power."

"Ya think?" I laughed dryly and let him tug me to my feet. My head spun, and I clutched both his arms to steady myself. "Where are we?"

"In my chambers. We were able to slip in undetected, but we mustn't keep Lucifer waiting any longer. Can you manage?" He stepped out of my grasp, and thankfully, I didn't topple.

"You live in Lucifer's palace?" I swept my gaze across the room. A chest of drawers in the same black wood as the couch stood against one wall, and a massive floor-to-ceiling window provided a view of the gothic gardens below.

"I did. We'll find out if I still do soon enough."

"What's the plan? You're obviously not going to offer me up to the devil, since our souls are connected. And I'm obviously not going to disconnect us since this bond is the only thing guaranteeing my safety." Not that I could undo it if I wanted to. Hopefully I could find some directions in the grimoire I had in my...

"Where's my backpack?"

"It's hidden. As for our plan, you must follow my lead. I can't predict Lucifer's mood nor his thoughts about my return. I will test the waters and decide from there. You must go along with whatever I say."

I crossed my arms. "The hell I must. Last time I followed your lead, I ended up bruised and burned inside a prison cell."

"We've established that keeping your soul intact is as important to me as it is to you. I am the only thing standing between you and complete obliteration, so I suggest you do as I say."

I pursed my lips, searching my mind for a witty comeback...or a better plan. I found neither. "Fine. We'll do it your way, but once we're out of this palace, you're returning my supplies and my weapons."

His lips twitched as if he were fighting a grin. "Done."

I started to demand he help me find my parents, too, but that was a merry-go-round of conversation I didn't care to have again. If I made it out of the palace alive...unobliterated...I might revisit it. For now, I'd glean as much information as I could about where bargained souls ended up in this goddess-forsaken realm, and then I'd find them myself.

"This way." He strode toward the wall and waved his hand in front of it. The sigils on the paper glowed, and a doorway appeared, revealing a set of stone steps that led downward into darkness. "After you."

I peered inside and shook my head. "Again, you're asking me to blindly step through a doorway when I have no idea what's on the other side. No way. After *you*."

"Do all women of your day and age despise chivalry, or is the quality unique to you?" He didn't wait for me to answer. The wall that once covered the opening began to shimmer back into place, so I rushed through, the sensation of claws ripping at my skin making me groan.

I stopped at the top of the stairwell to catch my breath. "You have got to stop expecting your magic not to affect me. I'm not going through any more magical wormholes."

"If you had gone in when I asked, it wouldn't have hurt." He continued his descent. "Your stubbornness caused you to pass through a partially materialized wall. You're lucky it didn't reform completely while you were inside it."

Against my better judgment, I followed him down. Not that I really had a choice. The doorway behind me was now a solid wall, so it was either follow him down or stay put, and I wasn't keen on testing whether the stairway would disappear after he descended it. "I'm a rogue soul in a realm where I don't belong. Excuse me for being cautious."

He waved his hand at the bottom, and another opening appeared. This one led outside, into the weird red-orange sunlight, and I brushed past him to get the hell out of that staircase. No way was I walking through a half-formed wall again.

"I'm surprised that word exists in your vocabulary. This way." He turned left and headed down a stone path running between the gardens and the palace.

If I'd had more time—and my soul wasn't in mortal danger—I could've spent hours exploring the grounds. Plants grew in Hell, believe it or not, their twisting, winding vines and deep purple flowers giving the place a gothic feel. Sculptures made of basalt and obsidian depicted animals and beautiful women, and towers of rocks in varying sizes balanced atop each other, defying the laws of physics.

"Why are we skulking around the side of the palace?" Despite the nearly hip-high slit in my dress, I couldn't take the strides of a woman on a mission. I had to scurry to keep up with him. I hated scurrying.

"Does your room not have a door on the inside?" I hiked up the dress as far as I dared, finally taking semi-normal steps.

He stopped at the split in the walk and held up a hand. "I have made nothing but mistakes since Isabel summoned me. I do not dare to waltz into a formal meeting as if I were never gone. Come."

He clutched my hand, and we rushed down the right-hand path toward a small arch in a stone wall. Well, he rushed.

I scurried like a squirrel. "Alright, Prince Pain In My Ass, I need you to slow down. You can't put me in a movement-restricting costume and expect me to keep up with your long-ass strides."

"Would you prefer I bend space again and drop you at the front door?" He kept walking.

"No, thanks."

"Then keep up."

We walked in silence for another minute or two before we crossed a foot bridge over a moat of lava. The viscous liquid bubbled and steamed beneath us, and I moved behind Discord so I could walk smack down the center. You'd think a bridge over a friggin' lava stream would have walls or handrails or something, but no.

Apparently, the kingdom of Hell didn't give a flying flip about OSHA regulations.

Safely on the other side of the bridge, we hung a left and made our way toward the main entrance. The palace was massive. Looking up at the spiraling turrets, I nearly lost my balance, stumbling before steadying myself with Discord's shoulder.

"Release your dress. You look like a harlot when you walk like that." He plucked my hand from his shoulder and adjusted his sleeves before smoothing the front of his jacket. "You are about to be in the presence of a god. Our situation demands reverence and class."

"First of all, no one says harlot anymore." I hiked the dress even higher.

He looked down his nose at me. "And second?"

I was about to launch into a speech about how sex workers deserved the same respect as any other person, but a rumbly blast that sounded like a foghorn emanated from the palace. The obsidian bridge glowed with red sigils, and Discord took off, crossing it without another word.

I scurried—once again—and followed him to the entrance. A set of polished wooden doors soared fifteen feet high, and the *thunk* of a lock disengaging sounded before two harpy-hounds pushed them open.

My heart tried to creep into my throat, so I swallowed hard. "Are those the same guys who threw me into your jail?"

"They are not." He touched the small of my back and ushered me inside, completely ignoring the dogs who'd opened the doors.

I turned my head, watching one as we passed. "They all look the same."

"It's a tendency of lower-level beasts."

"Whoa." I stopped short in the massive foyer, finally dropping my dress and spinning in a circle. A grand staircase rose in front of us before splitting three ways at the second floor, and a chandelier made of red glass and glowing—were those human bones?—hung in the center of the vaulted ceiling.

Seven arched doorways led to who knew where, and Discord gestured to the third on the right. "Follow my lead."

"Will do." I started to call him Captain of Crazy, but I deserved the title more than him, seeing as how I'd just waltzed into Lucifer's lair wearing a prom dress and combat boots.

The hallway twisted and turned for what felt like miles, and an ornate gilded arch stood at the end, opening into a ginormous throne room. Gold and red sigils glowed on the slate floor and walls, and people —demons in human form—milled about in formal attire.

I felt like I'd just stepped into a vampire ball in New Orleans…and I was to be their main course.

A long red carpet stretched from the entrance to a dais at the opposite end of the room, where the most polished, aristocratic man I had ever seen sat atop a throne of gold-encrusted bones. His black pinstriped jacket sported dark burgundy lapels, and his short hair was parted on the side and gelled perfectly into place.

"I never pictured Lucifer blond," I whispered.

"His appearance changes with his mood." Discord ushered me forward.

"Is blond good?" I adjusted the top of my dress, lest the sleeveless side give the King of Hell a glimpse of my goods.

"He is at ease for now." He took three more steps and bowed his head, lowering to one knee in front of the throne.

If I tried that in this dress, I'd never get back up. So I curtsied instead and looked him in the eyes. "It's a pleasure to meet you, Your Highness."

He narrowed his eyes, the icy blue turning stormy before he focused on Discord. "You may rise."

Discord straightened and cut me a sideways glance. Oh, yeah. I wasn't supposed to speak unless spoken to. Whoops.

Lucifer gave me a blasé once over, clearly unimpressed, before lifting his hand and signaling with two fingers in a come here motion. Two men came up behind me so quickly, I barely had time to register the shift in energy. They grabbed my arms, their super-uber-demonic strength pinning me to the spot.

"What the hell?" I struggled, but my arms might as well have been encased in concrete. These suckers were *strong*.

Discord glared at the men, growling low in his throat as he tensed and widened his stance. Another pair came at him, a man and a woman armed with black blades.

The woman lunged, striking out with a dagger toward my demon's side. Discord clutched her wrist, using her momentum to fling her across the room. The man swung a two-foot-long sword at Discord's neck, but he ducked, dodging the attack easily.

He grabbed the hilt of the sword with one hand and landed a punch in the center of the attacker's face with the other. Blood dripped from the man's nose as he stumbled away. The woman screamed like a banshee and leaped onto Discord's back, pressing a dagger against his throat.

He let out a slow breath, his expression completely bored, before he dropped backward to the ground, landing on top of the woman. Her head smacked the hard slate, and she grunted, releasing him.

Discord rose and rested a knee in the center of her chest. He snatched the dagger from her hand, flipping it before pressing the tip against the dip at the base of her neck.

"Enough," Lucifer finally said, and the men released me.

Discord rose to his feet and offered the woman a hand up. She accepted, nodding her appreciation, and then took a seat along the wall. The men joined her, and Discord straightened his jacket, smoothing the lapels and facing his king.

"I'm glad to see you haven't lost your battle skills." Lucifer placed his elbows on two femurs and steepled his fingers, resting his ankle atop one knee. "How long have you been home, my son?"

Discord ran a hand through his hair, though it wasn't disheveled in the slightest. "Two days at most, sire."

Two days? No wonder I was starving.

"At most?" Lucifer uncrossed his legs and leaned forward, his posture imposing enough to make me step backward. "You don't know?"

Discord cleared his throat and straightened his spine. "My concept of time waned with my imprisonment. I'm still adjusting."

"I see." Lucifer leaned back and re-steepled his fingers. "Has your concept of protocol also waned? You should have given me audience the moment you crossed the veil."

"My apologies." He bowed his head before looking at the devil. "I was in no shape to appear before you."

Lucifer regarded him for a moment before cutting his gaze to me. "And this witch. Is she the one who freed you?"

I straightened, holding my head high. "I am, and in exchange for returning him to you, I would like safe passage for myself and my parents to the earthly realm."

Discord growled softly beside me, and I clamped my mouth shut. Was I out of my ever-loving mind? Why those words crossed my lips, I couldn't say, but they were out there now. I might as well own them.

I squared my shoulders and infused my words with as much vim as I could. "A prince in exchange for three witches. It's a fair trade."

Lucifer's brows shot toward his hairline, surprise morphing his features before he recovered. His hair darkened at his temples, his jaw tightening, and Discord stiffened beside me. I took two full breaths before anyone moved.

Discord jutted out his arm, wrapping his fingers around my throat before stepping so close I could feel his breath on my face as he spoke. "You will not bargain with our king. You will not speak again unless you are asked. Is that clear?"

"Crystal," I wheezed, and he let me go.

Lucifer cut his gaze between us, and a chuckle

rolled up from deep in his chest. His hair returned to blond, and he let out a full-on belly laugh. "How I have missed you." He rose to his feet. "Join me in the dining room. We'll feast to your return. Then, we'll deal with your insolent witch."

CHAPTER II

DISCORD

Cinder wished for her soul to be shredded into oblivion. It was the only explanation my mind could comprehend. Why else would she be so bold? No, not bold. That wasn't the right word to describe her transgression. Stupid. Moronic. Imbecilic. She was lucky Lucifer hadn't struck her down in that instant.

We both were.

"You seem to forget my fate is tied to yours," I whispered as we followed a servant toward the dining room. "You're supposed to be following my lead."

"I might do that if you were actually leading. All you've done so far is grovel, put on a show, and kiss his ass. At least I'm moving the conversation forward." She brushed her hair behind her bare shoulder and shrugged dismissively. "If you have a plan, I'm all ears."

I blew out a sharp, irritated breath. "My plan was to test the waters. To only say as much as his mood allowed."

"His hair was blond. You said that meant he was happy, so I went with it."

We stopped outside the dining room doors, and as the servant opened them, I regarded Cinder. Perhaps bold was a good word for her. She'd seen an opportunity and taken it, and if she'd been speaking to anyone other than Lucifer himself, I'd have applauded her effort.

The servant gestured for us to enter, and we stepped inside. The grand table, which could easily seat thirty, was set for seven. The polished black granite gleamed beneath half a dozen candelabra made of gilded bones. Orange flames flickered in response to my magic...possibly to Cinder's as well... casting dancing shadows onto the walls, and ornate silver goblets sat beside black chargers etched with red veins that pulsed softly. Atop the chargers sat neatly folded black napkins with Lucifer's monogram embroidered in crimson thread.

Two harpies entered from a swinging door and tugged two chairs from beneath the table, their gazes cast downward as always when in the presence of royalty. We took our seats, and they exited the chamber, leaving me alone with the thorn in my side called Cinder.

"What's the plan, Captain?" She started to take the napkin from her charger, but I caught her hand and shook my head. If her mouth didn't get us both obliterated, her manners would.

"We accept Lucifer's hospitality with grace. Do not mention your demands again until he asks, and do not, for any reason whatsoever, reveal my mark on your arm or mention our blood bond."

"It's not much of a plan, but okay." She dropped her hands into her lap.

Another door opened, and four new members of the court sauntered in. I recognized Bedlam, Ruin, and Tumult immediately. They wore black suits with blood red shirts, and they'd all slicked their dark hair back in matching styles.

The woman accompanying them I had never seen before. She had silver hair, cropped short to her head, and she wore a dark blue satin pantsuit with nothing else beneath the jacket. If the seer hadn't shown me the changes of the past centuries, I'd have been appalled at her appearance. Now, it seemed women could wear whatever they chose, even in the earthly realm.

"The mighty Discord has returned." Bedlam pulled out a chair for the woman, tucking her in as she sat.

Arrogance seeped from his pores, and he laughed before taking a seat.

"And he brought a witch instead of his brothers." Tumult sat next to him. "What are we to think of that?"

Ruin let out a hard exhale as he took a seat. "You should have stayed across the veil."

"This witch has a name, and you will use it." I crossed my arms, straightening my back. "Cinder, meet Ruin, Tumult, Bedlam, and...?"

The woman tilted her head, her calculating gaze sliding over me before she focused on Cinder. Lucifer strode into the room, and the servants hurried in behind him. He positioned himself at the head of the table, and they filled our goblets with wine before placing the napkins in our laps.

As they returned to the kitchen to prepare our first course, Lucifer sipped his wine, eyeing Cinder over the rim of his goblet. A spark of possessiveness ignited in my chest. I instinctively leaned toward her and narrowed my eyes at him in warning.

He chuckled and set down his glass. "Four hundred years of sensory deprivation, and you haven't changed a bit."

"But I see your court has." I glanced at Ruin, who sat at Lucifer's immediate right...where I should have been.

"Someone had to pick up the slack while you were

out playing with witches." Ruin leaned forward in a feeble attempt to intimidate me.

"Believe me. He and I are not playing at anything," Cinder said.

"And she speaks for you as well." Ruin arched a brow, and I imagined my fist erasing the amusement from his face.

Sadly, Lucifer did not tolerate physical altercations at dinner, so I squeezed Cinder's knee beneath the table instead, hoping to remind her of our positions in this power play.

Ignoring Ruin's jab, I turned my attention to the silver-haired woman. "I don't believe you told me your name."

"You're right. I didn't." She sipped her wine and said no more.

Lucifer clucked his tongue. "That's no way to speak to our fallen prince. Tell him who you are."

She flicked her gaze to the king before inclining her chin. "My name is Seraphine Gale. I'm the most skilled hunter you will ever meet, and I am the *only* witch in Lucifer's court."

She looked at Cinder. "It will stay that way."

"There, there, Seraphine," Lucifer said, speaking as if the witch were a child. "Cinder isn't here to infiltrate us. Are you dear? No, she has her own agenda, I'm afraid."

Cinder's silver-tongue magic flared, but I squeezed

her knee once more before she could speak. Hecate had been the only witch in Lucifer's court for centuries. Her absence and apparent replacement were concerning. The goddess had always been the calm to Lucifer's storm.

The kitchen door swung open, interrupting the lethal conversation, and seven harpies entered, each carrying a silver-domed dish. They stood behind us, and as Lucifer nodded, they set the dishes down and removed the domes in unison, revealing a thick brown puree.

"Leek and shallot soup, seasoned with essence of gluttony and shame," the head servant said. "Enjoy."

"Gluttony and shame?" Cinder leaned toward me, lowering her voice. "Is it safe for me to eat here?"

"It would be unsafe if you didn't," I whispered.

"*Bene sapiat*," Lucifer said, lifting his glass before taking a sip and setting it on the table. "Enjoy your meal."

Cinder eyed her soup, and I could almost see the calculations forming in her mind. I picked up my spoon and dunked it into the salty liquid. Shame was an acquired taste, one I never appreciated, which Lucifer knew. Adding it to our first course was a not-so-subtle hint at my place in this realm. I took a bite, and Cinder followed my lead, her lips tightening as she swallowed.

"How do you like it?" Lucifer suppressed a smile as he watched Cinder take another bite.

She swallowed and dabbed the napkin to the corners of her mouth. "I've always said leeks are the most underrated vegetable. They're my favorite."

Good answer. Perhaps we might survive this dinner after all.

The second course consisted of skunk cabbage salad with a dressing made from the tears of the tormented. Cinder cringed when the harpy announced it, but she ate, nodding her head in false appreciation. *I could only imagine the nausea she must have felt with each bite.*

Seraphine wiped her mouth. "Tormented tears perfectly counter the sweetness of the cabbage. Don't you think, sire?"

"What do you think, dear Cinder?" Lucifer asked, making Seraphine clench her jaw.

Cinder swallowed and took a large drink of wine before answering, "I've always liked the combination of salty and sweet. Like salted chocolate or caramel. They complement each other well."

She smirked at Seraphine and took another bite, her gaze never straying as she chewed and swallowed. *Admiration warmed my chest, and I fought my smile. I never dreamed an earthly witch could be so skilled at underworldly diplomacy.*

The harpies cleared our salad plates and returned

with the main course. "A prime rib cut of Stygian steer with goose foie gras and garlic butter." They refilled our goblets and returned to the kitchen.

Cinder cut into her steak and took a bite. Surprise flashed in her eyes, and she nodded. "This is delicious."

"Hmm." Lucifer's gaze grew wistful. "It was Hecate's favorite."

"Was?" The question left my lips before I could temper it.

The hair at Lucifer's temples began to darken, and Seraphine shifted uncomfortably in her seat. Bedlam, Ruin, and Tumult took larger bites as if now rushing through their meals.

"Dinner first." Lucifer cut into the meat, tightening his grip on the knife, his movements growing aggressive.

Cinder tensed beside me, obviously aware of the shift, and she rested her hand on my thigh, tapping her index finger against my pants. I laid my hand atop hers, silently acknowledging the imminent danger.

Lucifer took a deep breath, and the darkness spreading through his hair stilled, leaving it dappled with black and blond. We ate in silence, though my appetite had diminished greatly, and the final course, a sweet blood pudding with a raspberry and turnip reduction, sat heavy in my stomach like a lump of basalt.

With the dishes cleared from the table, Lucifer leaned forward, folding his arms on the surface. "Tell me, Discord, how this situation came to be."

I straightened, casting Cinder a warning look to remain quiet before I began. "A powerful witch summoned Chaos, Mayhem, and me over four centuries ago. She promised her soul and that of her firstborn in exchange for cursing the Holland bloodline. We agreed, but her power was greater than we could have imagined."

Tumult chuckled, and Ruin rolled his eyes. Seraphine narrowed hers, clearly unamused by their dismissal of a witch's magic.

"She stole Hecate's amulet from me and vanquished us all to the dark prison," I continued. "There I remained until Cinder located my skull and summoned me."

He cut his gaze between the two of us, his silence making my muscles crawl beneath my skin. "Hecate left my court because of your misdeed." His hair turned solid black, taking all hope of parting as friends with it. "She left *me*."

"It was never my intention to—"

He held up his hand, stopping my apology. "No one has seen nor heard from her in centuries. I fished through the pool of damned souls for a witch strong enough to fill her shoes, but Hecate isn't only a witch. She's a goddess. Seraphine was the best I could find." He waved at her dismissively, and she tensed.

Leaning back in his chair, he rested his hands on the arms, his jaw moving slightly from side to side as he chose his words. "I helped Hecate forge that amulet. It was a symbol of our partnership, our union. I was in the doghouse for a decade when I lost it to you in that ill-fated bet. She saw it as a betrayal, and she never fully forgave me. Then, you lost it to a *mortal* witch."

I remained silent, staring straight ahead at Ruin's smug expression. Lucifer spoke the truth, and no amount of groveling would change the outcome of what I'd done.

"Tell me, Cinder," he said. "When you presented your bargain—a prince in exchange for three witches —were you aware of the shame he has brought to my court?"

She swallowed hard. "I knew why he was imprisoned. He didn't mention the part about Hecate or the amulet."

"I see." His jaw tensed. "So you believed I would be overjoyed at his return and would grant you and your parents safe passage to return to the earthly realm, despite the fact your parents sold their souls to the entity they summoned."

"Something like that." She forced a dry laugh. "To be fair, the demon they summoned didn't hold up his end of the bargain. He was supposed to deliver the princes before he dragged them to Hell."

Lucifer steepled his fingers. "I'm afraid my sense of fairness ran out when Hecate left me."

He studied her for a moment before shifting his attention to me. "Cinder didn't sell you her soul."

I ground my teeth. "She did not."

"It baffles me, truly, why you would bring an unclaimed mortal soul into our realm while leaving your brothers and the amulet behind. Unless..." He held up a finger. "Unless you've brought her to me as an offering. I sense her power is great, and with fire as her element... Well, you know how I love it when things get heated."

"She is not an offering." My hands curled into fists, and I leaned toward him, fighting to remain in my seat. The blood bond Cinder had created grew stronger with each passing second, making me more and more possessive of her. The thought of Lucifer...of anyone...touching her filled me with murderous rage.

"If you allow her safe passage home, she will find Chaos, Mayhem, and your precious amulet and return them to you."

Lucifer chuckled. Then he laughed heartily. "Your brothers are nearly as imprudent as you. They deserve their fate."

He drummed his fingers together. "Tell me, Discord. Do you take me for a fool?"

The bitter taste of bile crept up the back of my throat. "Of course not."

"Nor did I you." He folded his arms on the table, leaning forward once more, his voice growing deeper, more menacing. "You didn't bring her here willingly to bargain with me. She forged a blood bond and forced you to. Did you truly think you could hide that from me with a strip of fabric? I felt it the moment I summoned you."

Lucifer shot to his feet, his chair scraping across the stone floor as he stood. "You, Discord, have brought shame upon my palace yet again."

Cinder gripped my thigh, her nails digging into my muscles as my heart sprinted in my chest. I pried from her grasp and rose to look him in the eyes.

His nostrils flared at my challenging posture, his pupils tightening into thin slits as he rested his fingertips on the table's surface. "Let it be known I've put a bounty on both their heads. I've stripped his title, and the one who brings me both their skulls will take his place at my right side."

Ruin snapped his head toward Lucifer. "Your right side is where I belong, sire."

Lucifer cast him a sideways glance. "Then I suggest you join the hunt."

"There has to be something we can do." Cinder rose, her silver-tongue magic rolling out in full force.

"How can we make amends? Our lives must be worth something. Name your price."

Lucifer tilted his head, his left eye twitching as he regarded her. I couldn't tell if it was her magic affecting him or if he simply couldn't turn down a good bargain. "My price is this: Find Hecate and convince her to return. Succeed, and I'll consider sparing your lives."

Cinder crossed her arms. "We're going to need—"

"We accept your terms," I said before she could continue. "When do the games begin?"

A sinister smile curled his lips as he leaned toward us and whispered, "Run."

CHAPTER 12

CINDER

My heart hammering in my chest, I took two steps backward, around my chair. "Are you serious? Run...as in...run right now?"

Seraphine reached beneath the table before rising to her feet and brandishing a twelve-inch dagger with a wicked, twisted blade. "If you'd rather wait until I retrieve my crossbow..."

I snapped my gaze to Lucifer, laying my magic on thickly. "At least give us a head start so we can get out of the palace. Where's the fun in hunting when your prey is already trapped?"

Tumult's brow crumpled as my power took hold. "She makes a good point."

"I do love a challenge," Bedlam said.

Ruin narrowed his eyes. "I will revel in every

second of the hunt, and when I win a permanent place by Lucifer's side, there will be no doubt I am the only one worthy of this post."

Such a dramatic one, that Ruin. If I wasn't scared shitless, I'd have rolled my eyes. "What do you say, Lucifer? Six, seven hours?"

The devil arched a brow. "You have fifteen minutes."

I opened my mouth to argue we couldn't make it past the moat in that amount of time, but Discord grabbed my forearm.

"Let's go." The urgency in his voice made my pulse sprint even faster as he dragged me out the door.

I hiked up my ridiculously tight dress and did my best to match his strides, but he was half a foot taller than me. Yep, I ended up scurrying. Yet again. We made it to the foyer, or the grand entrance...whatever you called the ginormous imposing room at the front of the palace...and stopped beneath the glass and bone chandelier.

Discord glanced from the massive staircase to the front door and back again.

"I vote we put as much distance between ourselves and Lucifer's flying monkeys as we can." I tugged from his grasp and headed to the exit. "We need to find Hecate ASAP, and she's obviously not inside the castle."

He remained rooted to the floor. "They are not

monkeys, nor can they fly, but they will not be the only creatures hunting us. Leaving the palace will be suicide."

"So will staying." I took a few more steps toward the door. When he didn't move, I stomped toward him and grabbed his arm. "Look, you're reeling. I get it. Betrayal, power plays, hubris, yada, yada, yada. You can tell me all about it later, but right now, we need to jet before they kill us and our little dog too."

"What dog?" He finally moved his feet and strode with me to the door.

"It's pop culture. Don't worry about it." I grabbed the iron rings on the double doors and pulled, but the damn things must've weighed two tons each. They wouldn't budge. "A little help here?"

"The things you say make no sense." He grabbed a ring and hauled the door open.

"You'll get used to it." Heat blasted my cheeks as we stepped onto the portico, and the aromas of frankincense and sulfur assaulted my nostrils. We made our way down the obsidian steps, but instead of heading to the main bridge and crossing the moat, he guided me to the left, across the front lawn.

Well, lawn wasn't the right word. No ryegrass or fine fescue covered the rocky ground, but plenty of shrubbery with knotted, twisty stalks shot up from the cracks in the basalt. We hung a left at the corner of the palace and made our way past a steaming pool of orange water. Or maybe it was acid. I preferred not to find out.

Discord walked faster and faster, and I scurried like a baby pig running from the slaughterhouse. That simply would not do.

"Hold on. This dress is impossible." I stopped beneath a gnarled, leafless tree and leaned a hand against it to steady myself as I reached into my boot and retrieved the steak knife I'd swiped from Lucifer's table. Jabbing the blade into the fabric at mid-thigh, I sawed and ripped until my dress went from maxi to mini. It wasn't pretty, but at least I could take a normal step now.

Discord furrowed his brow as I returned the knife to my boot and dropped the dress scraps near the trunk. "I don't know whether to be impressed or appalled that you had the nerve to steal from Lucifer."

"You'll have time to clutch your pearls when we find Hecate." I jogged to catch up. No more scurrying for this bad bitch. "We need a place to hide and a plan. Weapons would be good too. Where's the bag you took from me?"

He glanced sideways at me and kept walking. "It's hidden."

"Good. Take me there. I can put on some sensible clothes and arm myself. Then we can discuss how to save ourselves from this predicament."

He stopped abruptly. "You are the reason we're in this predicament. You're in no position to bark orders."

I put a hand on my hip. "And you are?"

He grunted, fisting his hands and continuing his trek. "This is my realm. I'm familiar with the landscape and the laws. Are you?"

I ground my teeth, racking my brain for an argument. "Okay, that's a fair point. But I would feel more comfortable if I had my weapons, some pants, and my grimoire. Will you please take me to where you hid my stuff?"

"Where else did you think we were going?"

"I don't know because you don't tell me anything." I glared at him, he glared back at me, and we both continued on in silence, crossing a footbridge over the palace moat and venturing into a forest of thorny trees.

Skeletal trunks curved like crooked spines, their branches stretching upward and outward at broken angles like arms before thinning into long, bony fingers that reached for each other yearningly across the canopy.

The deeper we ventured into the woods, the weightier all my burdens became. The arbor thickened, the leafless branches growing denser above us until the shards of dappled orange light dancing across the ground extinguished and the atmosphere grew heavy and oppressive.

My chest tightened, my throat thickening as pressure built in the backs of my eyes. I choked on a sob, trying to stop the tears from falling, but the sense of hopeless anguish came on too quickly for me to fight it off.

What had my life come to? Seriously, look at me. There I was in *Hell*, traipsing through the Swamp of Sadness with The Demon Formally Known as Prince and playing a high-stakes game of hide-and-seek with the local hunters who wanted my skull so they could become second in command to the devil himself.

What. The. Actual. Eff?

Another sob rolled up from my throat. I covered my mouth, but I couldn't stop it. My chest heaved, and I gave in to the sorrow, allowing it to wash over me, to drag me under. I couldn't walk. Couldn't move. Nothingness consumed me. I'd gotten myself into the pickle of all pickles, and there was nothing left for me to do but drown in the brine.

Discord growled beside me, as if the sound could ward off the overwhelming despair. "The forest is affecting you."

"It's okay. You go find Hecate. I'll just lie down right here." I bent, reaching for the ground.

"Do that, and Lucifer will turn your skull into a goblet." He clutched my hand. "We have to keep moving."

I tried to tug from his grasp, but he held me

tighter, pulling me to his chest. It wasn't a hug. He was a demon for Hecate's sake, so I knew he was only holding me to keep me from falling to the ground, but he was warm and firm, and the embrace turned my waterworks up to full power. "Why...delay the...inevitable?" I asked between sobs.

"I have no intention of going down without a fight, and I know you don't either." He scooped me into his arms and carried me. "This forest was grown from the bones of desperate souls, those willing to pay any price to end their suffering or that of a loved one."

"How awful." I sobbed even harder and buried my face in his shoulder. "Why would anyone want to grow a forest out of that?"

"For exactly this reason." He adjusted his grip to lift me over a fallen log. "Anyone attempting to approach the palace from the north would have to pass through the Forest of Suffering Souls. As you've learned, it's virtually impenetrable. Most who've attempted it have lain down and died."

I lifted my head to see his face. Not a single tear wet his cheek. "Why can you get through it?"

"I'm one of the most powerful demons in the realm, and until today, I was Lucifer's faithful servant. My fealty, combined with my magic, granted me immunity."

"Oh." I cast my gaze to the rocky ground and hiccup-sobbed at the sight of skeletons strewn about.

Squeezing my eyes shut, I pressed my face against his shoulder and cried even more.

"Those who perished here planned to infiltrate the palace. To usurp Lucifer and steal his throne." He turned away from the carnage. "But that was a long, long time ago."

This forest had to be the most goddess-awful place I had ever been. As Discord carried me through it, stepping over logs and roots and who knew how many scattered bones, I honestly didn't care if we ever made it out. Everything seemed pointless. Hopeless. Futile beyond measure.

But after a while—whether it had been thirty minutes or thirty days, I couldn't say—the pressure in my chest lightened. The air didn't feel quite as thick as I raked it into my lungs, and the darkness I had been wishing would devour me started to lighten.

The thick, spindly branches thinned, and red-orange light pierced the canopy. I sucked in a shaky breath, then another, testing whether I could go ten seconds without sobbing uncontrollably. I looked straight ahead at the clearing in the distance, not daring a glimpse of the ground. I couldn't bear to see another shattered bone.

When we reached the tree line, Discord stopped and cupped my cheek in his hand, turning my face to meet his gaze. "We've reached the forest edge. Are you strong enough to continue the journey?"

I expected to see annoyance in his eyes, or even a smugness that he could make it through that horrible, awful, very bad place when I was ready to become its next victim. Instead, I was met with compassion, and if I didn't know any better, I'd say he blinked back unshed tears.

"I think... Yeah, umm..." I wiggled out of his embrace, and he lowered my feet to the ground. My dress had gotten hiked up too high for my comfort, so I shimmied it down and made sure my girls were in their proper places.

I swear I heard him sniffle as I adjusted my clothes, but when I looked at him, the only evidence of tears I could find was mine, along with my snot, smeared all over his lapel. I rubbed my hands over my face and wiped my nose on my sleeve.

His lips twitched, tugging into a smile on one side. "All good?"

"I will be." I hiccupped, and the last of my tears rolled down my cheek. "That was intense."

His eyes grew misty, and he swallowed hard. "We need to keep moving."

"Wait a second." I grabbed his hand before he could walk away. "It affected you too, didn't it?"

He scoffed. "No. I'm Prince of Hell, I—"

"You *were* a prince. Now you're just a demon, and you teared up. Are *you* all good?"

As he took a deep breath, his gaze locked with

mine. The sigil on my arm heated, and it felt like we were opposing ends of a magnet, completely opposite in every way, yet drawn together by a force too powerful to fight. My body drifted toward him, the incredible urge to take his face in my hands and kiss him overpowering me.

Thankfully, my feet stayed firmly in place, and I blinked, snapping out of that alternate reality where I was falling for a demon. *Whew.* It was the trauma bond. It had to be because light witches and dark demons did not mix. Ever.

He cleared his throat. "I believe our blood bond caused me to feel your emotions. I'm fine, but we must keep moving. This way."

He kept a firm grip on my hand, and we skirted the tree line, heading toward a town on the horizon. Sometimes it felt like we'd been walking for hours, but when I focused on the sensation, it seemed only minutes had passed. The orange ball in the sky didn't seem to move, so it had to be minutes.

"Is that a sun or a moon?" I asked. "It's been like twilight the entire time I've been here."

"It is the moon. The sun never shines in Hell."

"How long have we been walking?"

He stopped abruptly, tugging me behind a tree as a pair of harpy-hounds passed overhead. "It's hard to say. Time isn't as linear here as it is on Earth, and my period away has made it difficult to comprehend. The forest's energy-draining power didn't help either. Let's keep moving."

He dropped my hand and peered at the sky. When the harpy-hounds disappeared into the horizon, we paced forward, leaving the so-called safety of the tree line. Even just walking close to it made me feel icky, so I can't say I minded losing our cover too much.

Finally, after who knew how long away from the Forest of Suffering Souls, the last of the sadness drained from my system. I furrowed my brow as we continued our trek toward the town, a spark of anger replacing the despair that almost unalived me.

"If you knew the effect that place has on people, why did you drag me into it? You knew it could kill me."

He glanced at me. "Technically, you're already dead."

"You know what I mean."

"You're a Holland witch. If you were as strong as you claimed to be, you would have been fine."

I scoffed. "I have never claimed to be any stronger than I am. That place kills *demons*. I don't buy it for a minute that you thought I'd be okay. Were you trying to kill me?"

He glanced again, arching a brow. "Perhaps I was teaching you a lesson."

I gave him a sideways glare. "And what lesson would that be?"

"That you're out of your element here, and you need me to survive. I chose that route because of its danger. The only safe way off the palace grounds is through the front. The hunters would assume I took you that way because every other route would likely obliterate you."

My jaw clenched. "First of all, I do not need you to survive. I've gotten along just fine without you for thirty years."

He laughed dryly. "In the earthly realm. Hell is different."

"You're ruled by an evil, narcissistic tyrant whose brainwashed minions stroke his ego and help him get away with whatever he wants. If you have laws, they sure as shit don't apply to him. Believe me, it's not that different."

"And your second point?"

"Second, next time we have a choice of challenges that'll likely kill me, I'd rather battle a boss-level dragon than take an emotional hit like that."

"I know."

"Then why didn't we go another way?"

"Because Lucifer and his 'brainwashed minions' know that too. Your demeanor makes your preference obvious, so I chose the least likely route." He jerked his head to the left, indicating I should follow him down an alley.

We entered the town, and he picked up his pace. "I

believed our blood bond would protect you. I thought I could share my immunity to the forest, but the bond works both ways. Your pain numbed my resistance. I didn't intend for you to suffer."

"Is that an apology?"

"No."

I followed him down the alley, and we made a right at the first corner. The squat buildings here were made of clay bricks and mud, the streets of cobblestone and rubble...a stark contrast to the city he'd taken me to before. Aside from the humid heat and sulfurous stench, it felt like we'd stepped into a sixteenth-century English town, frozen in time.

He stopped at the next corner and peered right then left. "Your bag is in the house two blocks ahead."

An air raid siren wailed from somewhere above. Or maybe it was below. Hell, it sounded like it came from all around me and inside my head at the same time, chilling me to the marrow. Discord's hands curled into fists, and the tendons in his neck tightened.

His reaction made my heart dip into my stomach, and I bit the inside of my cheek. I knew we were screwed, but I just had to ask anyway. "What does that mean?"

He let out a slow breath. "It means the hunt is on."

"Well, shit."

CHAPTER 13

DISCORD

"**I** suggest we run." I leaned forward, checking the streets for adversaries, but Cinder took my suggestion without hesitation. She darted toward my secret residence, leaving me no choice but to follow.

The siren still blaring, we slipped inside before the locals could decipher the signal. Cinder went for the light switch, but I caught her hand, holding it tightly as the message blasted through my psyche, filling my mind with the rules of the game and information about the bounty.

She swayed and clutched her head. "Holy mother of magic. Ouch."

"Everyone in the realm now knows we're fugitives." I removed my mucus-stained jacket and paced to the closet before tossing it onto the floor. The clothing here, though magically preserved, was four centuries old and out of fashion, but what did it matter? I was an outlaw in my own land.

I grabbed a pair of pants from a shelf and shook them out. The coarse fabric didn't stretch at all, and its roughness made the clothes I currently wore feel like butter against my skin. I sighed and dropped the pants on top of my discarded jacket. It appeared I'd be on the run in formal attire.

Cinder took off her boots and swung her bag over her shoulder. "Where can I change?"

I pointed to the bathroom, and she stepped inside, kicking the door behind her. It didn't close all the way, leaving me an obstructed view of her as she undressed. She tugged the shredded dress over her head, and blood rushed to my groin. It seemed Belira had neglected to lend her any undergarments.

She bent down and stepped into the satiny swath of fabric I'd found in her pack. My, how underwear had changed over the centuries. My dick hardened, and I licked my lips before turning around and beating a fist against the wall.

Before my thoughts had turned to a hollow void in the dark prison, I had vowed that I would never associate with a witch again. My hatred and distrust of Cinder's kind hadn't waned, yet I found myself inexplicably drawn to her.

The desire to protect her, to provide for her, and to

make her my own overwhelmed me. It had to be the blood bond fabricating these emotions. She had done nothing but cause me pain and strife from the moment she resurrected me, and I would take pleasure in her demise if only it wouldn't mean my own ending as well.

A growl rumbled in my chest, the anger that consumed me shifting its focus to myself. How could I have let this happen? I replayed the moment she vanquished me in my mind. She'd moved quickly, plunging the dagger into my heart without considering the consequences.

I had let my guard down, assuming her self-preservation instinct would force her to consider my vanquishment meant her death. It appeared that was an instinct she lacked.

Cinder was rash, single-minded, arrogant, and bold. Her impulsiveness put us both in danger every time she opened her mouth, and I couldn't help but admire her for all those qualities and more.

I was a fool.

"Where's my grimoire?" she asked from behind me, and I turned around to find her fully clothed in black pants and a dark gray shirt. She set her bag on a chair and rested a hand on her hip, drawing my attention to her curves.

My hands fisted of their own accord. "I traded it to the seer for a glimpse of the past four hundred years."

"You used my spell book to pay for a history lesson?" Her expression was incredulous. "Couldn't you have watched a few documentaries on the Discovery Channel? I need it back."

"I'm afraid it's gone, and we have more pressing matters to deal with. We're being hunted...or have you forgotten?" I opened a panel in my closet wall and retrieved a leather satchel.

Cinder glared, pursing her lips. "Fine. What's the plan? Whose house is this? Another ex-girlfriend?"

I set the satchel on the table and loosened the drawstring. "This residence is mine."

"I thought you lived in the palace." She crossed her arms.

"Officially, I do."

"You mean did."

I blew out a hard breath and took a hunting knife with an eight-inch blade from the bag. "Before I was imprisoned, I officially resided in the palace. Lucifer, as you have learned, can be intense. I built this home as a secret residence where I could escape to seclusion when I needed it."

I laughed dryly at the memory and set down the knife. "I used to crave solitude. I was created to instill conflict and disagreement in everyone around me, but even the essence of discord itself gets tired of the ruckus."

"I get it." She picked up the knife and examined the

blade, weighing it in her hand. "You were the devil's right hand, but sometimes you have to be your own man."

I flicked my gaze to her eyes, expecting to be met with ridicule. My desire for solitude, my need for separating myself from the position I was created to perform, was a weakness at best. Some would even call it my fatal flaw.

She met me with compassion and understanding. "Before all this, I was being groomed to take over as High Priestess of Salem. But something about it doesn't sit right. There has always only ever been one, and when it comes time for me to be that person, I'll have to be prepared to shoulder it all on my own."

"And you aren't ready to accept the challenge." I took a thigh holster from the bag and strapped it on.

"I would have been, if my parents hadn't done what they did. I was learning to do it all on my own, but it always felt so...lonely." She held my gaze for a moment before blinking rapidly and shaking her head. "Anyway. Being High Priestess is my birthright, so I'll figure it out. Being hunted like wild game in Hell, I did not sign up for."

"And I did?" I yanked the strap on my holster, narrowing my eyes, her final words needling me. "What did you think would happen when you bound yourself to a demon and vanquished us both? Did you expect me to drop to my knees and kiss your feet? To magically know where your parents were and be willing to send you all across the veil with a flick of my wrist?"

"Something like that." She shrugged. "Look, I didn't expect unicorns shitting rainbow sherbet, but I figured you'd have some pull since you're...you were...a prince and all."

I huffed and continued strapping on my weapons. Cinder opened her bag and did the same.

"You do realize you're dead, I hope. Your parents too." I tossed the empty weapon bag into the closet. "Your strength allowed you to maintain your corporeal form when you crossed the veil, but unless you have a necromancer on the other side, you cannot go back alive without Lucifer's blessing. Lucifer's... The man who just put a price on our heads."

She drummed her fingers on the back of a chair. "I'm sure there's another way."

"Are you?"

Her jaw tightened. "First things first. Let's find Hecate. I'll get her to forgive you and Luci, and I'll convince her to return to the palace. You'll get back in his good graces, and then we'll go from there. Maybe Hecate can send me home."

"You make it sound so easy."

"Like a Sunday morning." She slung her bag over

her shoulder, a look of confusion contorting her features. "Wait. If you knew you were headed to your secret house here, why did you drag me through that forest? Why didn't you do your little space-bending thing and bring us right here?"

"With the way you reacted last time, a jump that far might have killed you."

Her lips quirked into a teasing smile. "I thought you said I'm already dead."

"Obliterated you. Decimated your soul. You know what I mean." I focused on my mark emblazoned on her arm, and it glowed softly in response. "It is in my best interest to keep you in your current state of existence, remember?"

She looked at her arm and ran a finger over the sigil, making my entire body hum as if she'd wrapped me in silk. "Then it's in my best interest to keep this baby here as long as possible."

"Indeed." I opened a cabinet and dialed the code to my safe. Inside lay three stacks of ashmarks. I took them all and handed one to Cinder.

"What's this?" She tilted her head, examining the bills made of magically flexible obsidian. Their denominations were marked in ancient sigils, and red veins pulsed through them as if they were alive.

"Ashmarks. Money. We'll need it to buy food and supplies on our journey." I shoved a stack into each pocket. "Can you cast a cloaking spell to change your appearance?"

She put the ashmarks into a small pouch on the front of her bag and crossed her arms. "I might have been able to if I had my grimoire. Spells like that require potions."

"You don't have one memorized?"

"I've never needed one."

"At the very least, I will change mine." I turned toward the mirror and focused on my face, allowing my magic to build in my chest before forcing it upward. My skin heated and tingled as it should have, but my appearance did not change.

"You still look the same to me," she said.

I tried again, focusing harder, squeezing my eyes shut.

"Now you just look constipated," Cinder said.

I opened my eyes and blew out a hard breath. "It appears some of my powers were stripped along with my title."

"Well, that's frigging fantastic."

"Not in the slightest." My stomach soured, my fury finding a new culprit to focus on.

"I was Lucifer's right hand for eons, his most trusted advisor, his confidant...his friend. This bounty he's placed, the stripping of my title and my powers, is nothing short of betrayal. And all this over a woman? It's unfathomable."

"Not really." Cinder stepped toward a window, pulling the curtain aside to peer out. "Love makes people do crazy things...like curse an entire bloodline."

Lucifer had been in love with Hecate. I knew that because he had confided in me about their relationship many times. But to completely uproot his court... to ask for his right hand's head on a stake...all because of a woman scorned?

"If she meant that much to him, he never should have wagered the amulet," I said.

She shrugged. "Maybe he thought there was no way he could lose."

"We must find her."

"Pretty sure that's been our plan since the game began." She stepped to the side, dropping the curtain and peeking through a slit. "How many people know this is your house?"

"None." I stepped behind her and peered out the opening in the curtain, where a throng of mid-level demons fanned out around the front of the building.

"It looks like a few dozen or so just figured it out," she said. "Got a back door?"

"This way." I paced down the hall with Cinder on my heels. When we reached the exit, I checked the window and held up a hand to stop her from barging out the door.

Six shedims blocked our escape.

"How do you think they found us?" Cinder peered

out, curling her lip at the sight of them. With their cracked charcoal skin, flat noses, and jagged teeth dripping with black drool, they appeared grotesque even to me.

"They sense my energy. Mid- and lower-level demons are drawn to my power. Before I became a fugitive, they would also do my bidding."

"And you didn't think to cloak your so-called secret house?" She scoffed. "I'm surprised no one found you here before."

"I had it cloaked. The magic has apparently worn off." I ground my teeth. "Would one of your spells last four hundred years?"

She pursed her lips. "Maybe."

The front door rattled, and the *bang* of a shoulder smacking the surface reverberated through the building.

"Shedims have two hearts in the center of their chests." I clutched my longest dagger in my hand. "You must pierce both to decimate them."

"Got it." Cinder opened her bag and rummaged through it.

The front door cracked. The demons outside howled.

"We must go now," I said.

"Okay." She retrieved an envelope before positioning the backpack on her shoulders and buckling it at her waist. "I'm ready."

I gripped the doorknob, and every muscle in my body tensed. "If you die in the Underworld, your soul will be obliterated. There is no coming back. Not even Lucifer can will it."

"You worry about you." She slid a hunting knife from its scabbard. "I can take care of myself."

I hoped to Hades she was right.

CHAPTER 14

CINDER

I meant it when I said I could take care of myself. Give me six vampire ghouls at once and I'd kill them all, no problem. Fae mosquitos? Call me the witch bug zapper because those babies were getting burned to a crisp. Fighting the beasties that could make it to my side of the veil was usually easy-peasy.

I had forgotten, however, that witch fire had zero effect on this side. Why would it? Streams of literal lava meandered through town like babbling brooks. I bet the shedims were planning a picnic on the rocky bank when they got through with us.

Too bad we were going to be through with them first.

Discord flung the back door open and charged toward the shedims. In his human form, he stood about six feet four. The would-be assassins towered at least half a foot over him, which meant they probably saw me as about as threatening as a cockroach.

Four of them swarmed Discord while the other two sneered at me, their thin lips peeling back to reveal jagged teeth with chunks of Hecate knew what lodged along their gumlines. I had no intention of letting them add my flesh to the rot, but hey, if they won this scuffle, at least they could use my hair as floss.

"Standing tall or on your—" *Oof.* The shedim charged so quickly, I barely noticed the blur of movement before it smacked into me. I careened backward, landing on the ground and hitting my head on a rock with a *thwack.*

Pain shot from the back of my skull to my eye sockets, making my vision swim. I squeezed my eyes shut, blinking them open in time to see the demon's claws glinting in the moonlight as they swiped toward my face.

The envelope filled with powdered binding spell had skidded across the rocks when I fell, but I still clutched my dagger tightly in my right hand. I slashed, slicing into the shedim's wrist. The force of my thrust knocked his claws away, sparing me from the wicked scars he'd attempted to make.

It did not spare me from getting a face full of demon blood, however. Thankfully, my mouth obeyed the command from my brain and kept my lips tightly shut. I did not want to know what this nasty sucker tasted like.

The shedim wailed and raised its other arm. I jabbed my dagger into the fiend's chest, twisting it and slicing up and down to make sure I got both hearts. Its eyes widened. If it had a human face, I'd have said the expression was a mix of incredulous and downright terrified.

Then it exploded.

Demon guts went everywhere.

My stomach lurched at the rancid stench of decay and garbage, but I managed to scramble to my feet in time to see Discord take out another one. That left four to contend with. I was certain the guys breaking into the front of the house wouldn't be far behind.

Switching my dagger from hand to hand, I inched backward toward the lava bank where the potion envelope had landed when I fell. The demon matched my strides, sizing me up as it snarled.

The rocky terrain tested my balance. My ankle rolled again, but I recovered. One of Discord's attackers screeched, drawing my shedim's attention, and I lunged for the envelope. My boot slipped on a patch of smooth obsidian, and I went down, catching myself with my hands and knocking the envelope farther toward the lava stream.

The corner hung over the edge, and it ignited, hellfire threatening to consume the last of my spell. I scrambled toward it. The demon charged. I flipped onto my back, bending my knees and kicking out, planting both boots in the demon's stomach and knocking him back.

"Get them," a deep, menacing voice ripped through the air.

I snapped my gaze toward the house and found the mob from the front door barreling out while one man stood on the porch, his arms crossed, his stance wide. He wore black cargo pants and a matching tank over his human form, and he inclined his chin, looking down at us as if he were Emperor Commodus, ready to give his gladiators the thumb down.

I grabbed the half-burned envelope and poured what was left of the charred powder into my hand. The Shedim charged again. I recited the incantation at warp speed and threw the powder at the beast.

It didn't freeze.

The fire must've changed the chemical makeup of the potion. The demon wrapped its claws around my throat and lifted me from the ground. My feet dangling, I clutched its hand and kicked, but it only squeezed me tighter.

"Discord," I rasped.

He whirled toward me, his expression livid. Three more of Commodus's lackies descended on him, trying to drag him to the ground. He fought back, landing a punch on one guy's jaw that ripped it from its socket. Even with his mandible hanging loose, the frigging demon continued his attack.

Another guy hit Discord with an uppercut while yet another kicked him in the gut. The shedim holding me looked to its master, and the guy *actually* gave him the thumb down gesture as if we were in the movie.

It looked like the monsters might get to use my hair as floss after all, dammit.

The shedim grabbed a handful of my locks, and my pulse sprinted. I whispered a prayer to the goddess that I'd pass out from lack of oxygen before it ripped my head from my body. Black drool dripped from its teeth, the stench of its sulfurous breath making my stomach turn. It snarled, opening its mouth like it was ready to chomp my face.

I'm sorry, Ash. I squeezed my eyes shut, unable to suck in another breath. I wouldn't say my entire life flashed before me in that moment...only everything I'd ever done wrong and every regret I'd ever had. I was the oldest sister. The next in line to lead our coven. The entire town was counting on me to end the curse, and I had failed them. I'd made one mistake after another during this entire ordeal, and...

The shedim wheezed, and I squinted blearily. Its eyes bugged, and it loosened its grip enough for me to drag in a breath. Its grip loosened more, and I scrambled away, gasping and coughing.

The demon exploded. Its guts blasted out in every direction, and two arrows fell into the heap of goo.

Another arrow whizzed by my head, landing in the center of a demon's chest. Thankfully, this guy didn't explode, because I couldn't handle swimming through any more gelatinous innards. He turned blue and then crumbled into ashes instead.

"Cinder!" Discord grabbed my arm. "Run."

Before I could make my feet move, an arrow clipped my shoulder. Searing pain ripped through my arm, jerking me into action. My boots pounded the rocks, adrenaline—and maybe the remnants of Ash's speed sigil—powering my strides as I pumped my legs, matching Discord's pace, my lungs heaving in the oppressive heat.

"This way," he said.

We hung a left down a narrow alley, darting behind a row of two-story buildings and slowing our pace, but my heart kept up its sprint, thanks to the adrenaline still surging through my system.

My shoulder screamed, reminding me how much the Underworld amplified pain. I'd had cuts before, bigger and deeper ones, but this felt like someone had sliced me open and sprayed liquid nitrogen into the wound.

"Where are we going?" My chest tightened and my head spun, so I leaned against a wall to steady myself. "I need to sit down."

"We have to keep moving." He took three long strides before turning around.

I must've looked like death warmed over because his expression went from determination to horror to anger in two seconds. He strode toward me, gingerly taking my arm and lifting the torn sleeve from my shoulder. He winced, but I didn't dare look to see why. Most of the blood from my head had already plummeted to my feet. I didn't need to push it.

"This isn't from the shedim." He placed his palm over the sigil and inhaled deeply, focusing on healing my injured shoulder, I assumed.

"Someone got me with an arrow." I leaned my head against the wall and closed my eyes.

"Poisoned with hoarfrost root. It's toxic to all who are born of fire and can turn them to ice."

"I guess that includes fire witches. Can you fix me like you did before?" The freezing pain shot down to my elbow, triggering the funny bone nerve, and I groaned, opening my eyes.

"I cannot. We must get you to the seer before..." His breath came out in a mist, as if it were below thirty.

"Before?"

He lifted his hands. The color in his fingers receded, turning them white from the tips to his palms. "We must both get to the seer. Can you walk?"

I pushed from the wall, squeezing my eyes shut as

the world spun. My stomach flipped, but I opened my lids and managed to stay upright. "How far?"

"The cave just beyond that stream." He pointed, and whiteness crept up his arm, freezing him to his shoulder.

"Looks like I have no choice." I headed in the direction he indicated, and he trudged behind me.

We passed another row of buildings with crumbling bricks and lopsided windows. The farther we got to the edge of town, the more dilapidated the structures became until they gave way entirely to leafless trees, mounds of stones, and a crushed basalt trail leading toward the cave.

"We're about to be out in the open here." I paused at the edge of the last building and rested my hand against a splintered piece of wood. What kind of trees grew in this sulfurous air and moonlight I had no clue, but there would be time for questions later. I hoped.

At the moment, my biggest concern was my swimming vision and the frostbite stretching from my collarbone to the middle of my forearm. That *was* my biggest concern, anyway...until I turned around.

Discord stood behind me, both his arms icy-blue and tinged with black lattice. The unnatural color stretched across his left shoulder and climbed his neck to spiral in a wave pattern over his cheek. Just a hint of blue fanned out on the right side of his neck, but with the way he stood, hunched to one side, I imagined the magically frostbitten infection had cascaded down his ribcage, making him unable to stand fully upright.

"Where did they get you?" I scanned his form for a bloody wound or torn fabric where an arrow might have pierced his skin.

"Didn't." He gave his head a tiny shake and grimaced. The left side of his mouth didn't move. "No time. Go alone."

"Those shedims must've knocked you upside the head pretty hard. I am not leaving you here to freeze." I grabbed his arm, ready to pull him down the trail, but his skin was so cold that it burned my hand.

"Ouch!" I jerked away.

"Go," he ground out.

"Not without you."

"You have to." His upper lip turned completely blue.

"You don't get to tell me what to do." I crossed my arms and jutted out a hip. "You need healing more than I do."

He growled, and the black lattice stretched to his nose.

I arched a brow.

He narrowed his right eye—the entire left side of his face had frozen solid—and he took a step and a half toward me. His right leg froze mid-stride, and he tipped over like an action figure that was posed wrong.

He hit the ground with a grunt before letting out the deepest, most agonizing groan I had ever heard.

"Discord!" I kneeled beside him, my racing heart now thrumming in my throat.

"Go alone," he managed to scratch out before his bottom lip turned blue too.

"Not a chance." My freezer burn spread down to my wrist, and one side of my neck began to stiffen. I bit my lip and scanned my surroundings for a tarp or a blanket or an adult-sized baby sling. Anything that would help me drag his heavy, frozen ass to the cave.

"Wait here," I said as if he had a choice, and I crept down the side of the building. A six-foot window with two busted panes occupied the center of the shack, and a brown curtain hung on the other side.

I hoped to Hecate the place was abandoned because I unhooked my backpack and slammed it into another pane, shattering the glass to reach the curtain. One good, hard yank tore it from half the rings, and I wrapped it around my good arm to pull it the rest of the way down before hightailing it back to my demon.

My stomach dropped into my boots when I found him. The icy skin on the side that hit the ground was cracked. If he froze any more solid, he might shatter.

"Shit. Shit, shit, shit." I dropped to my knees and worked the curtain beneath him while I still had use of both my hands. "Why is it affecting you so much faster? How many times were you hit?"

He didn't answer.

I lifted his shoulders and slid the curtain beneath him. Then I lay him down and rolled him to one side, working the drapery beneath him until most of his weight was situated on the fabric. His boots would drag the ground, but this would have to do.

I tied the free end of the curtain to my backpack and buckled it into place before heaving forward like a sled dog. My stomach roiled and my head spun, but I plowed ahead, my leg muscles burning with the exertion as I trudged down the gravel path.

The air was still, the entire area way too quiet for my liking. The posse of demons who'd attacked us at the house hadn't followed. Had the mysterious archer killed them all? Was someone in this goddess-forsaken realm actually on our side?

If so, why would they shoot at me? Maybe it was an accident. Maybe they were aiming for another demon. Maybe, maybe, maybe... My thoughts swirled and spiraled until I couldn't hold on to any of them. Just a little bit farther, and we'd be at the cave entrance.

My legs trembled, my neck and upper back going completely stiff from the poison. I opened my mouth, but one side of my face had gone numb. I didn't dare look back at Discord. I was still here, so that meant there was at least a little life left in him. That was enough for me.

"Hello?" I called into the cave. Beaded curtains that looked an awful lot like bones hung in the entrance, and I pushed through, dragging my demon into the...foyer? What did you call the entrance to a cave?

"Excuse me? Is there a seer who lives here? We need her help." I unbuckled my backpack and slid it off my good arm first and then the frozen one. "We need an antidote for hoarfrost poison. I'm afraid we're turning to ice."

"Enter, child." Two distinct voices spoke in unison, one deep and gravelly, the other almost melodic.

"Please, I can't pull him any farther." My side ached, the muscles tightening as the poison spread.

Another curtain of bones rattled, and a woman in a long black gown stepped through. Her right side appeared normal, almost human, with fair skin and a brown eye. The other half looked like she'd either stood too close to a volcano or she'd found the Arc of the Covenant along with the Nazis in *Indiana Jones*.

She stood in front of me, a white sheen clouding her left eye, and tilted her head as she examined my skin. I could only imagine how I must've looked. Possibly a bit like her.

"It's Discord. He's almost gone. Please help him." I shuffled toward him, trying to kneel by his side, but my freezing body wouldn't allow me to bend.

"Discord..." she mused.

"Yes, I know. I know there's a price on our heads, but the game has only just begun. We haven't had a chance. We…" My jaw tightened, my brows growing heavy over my eyes.

"Everything in Hell comes at a price." She folded her hands over her stomach and returned her gaze to me.

"I'll pay whatever you want. There's a stack of ashmarks in my bag. Just, please save us. Save him."

"I will help you." She pulled the bone curtain aside, beckoning me deeper into the cave. "Him, I cannot save."

CHAPTER 15

CINDER

"You don't understand. We're linked." I dragged myself through the bone curtain, my boot scraping across the obsidian floor with each step. I could no longer bend my knee.

"I understand clearly. Lie down." She gestured to a bed in the back corner before stepping toward a cauldron hanging above a fire. An enclave had been carved into the stone, making it look like the open fire ovens from way back when, and she used a rag to swing the pot toward her, away from the flames.

I would've loved to do as she asked. To just lie down, close my eyes, and sleep for a few centuries. But my frozen muscles wouldn't allow it. "I can't."

She looked at me with sympathy in her good eye, and she padded barefoot toward me. "I do this in exchange for the kindness he has shown me."

She chanted something in an ancient tongue. My Latin was rusty at best, but this didn't sound anything like it. The gravelly half of her dual voice seemed to slither over me, wrapping around me like a snake, while the melodic half tingled on my skin, making me feel lighter and lighter until my feet literally left the floor.

With one hand on my shoulder and the other beneath my leg, she lifted me *light as a feather, stiff as a board* style and floated me onto the mattress. Holy Hecate on a bicycle. I needed to learn how to do that.

"Where is your payment?" she asked.

"In my bag out front. Take however much you need. Take it all." I turned my head toward her, and my neck froze in place. "He's in worse shape than I am. Please help him."

"There is nothing I can do for him." She pulled the bone curtain aside and stepped into the foyer, leaving me alone with my burning, frozen body and my thoughts.

The whole if-he-died-I-died thing aside, I felt horrible about his condition. Every slight twitch of my muscles was incredibly painful, so I could imagine the amount of agony he must've been in. I closed my eyes and pondered everything that had happened.

He was a demon, one of the three responsible for my family's curse. He was the reason Ash's life—everyone in the coven's lives—were on the line. If we weren't connected, if I could survive his death, would I be so desperate to save him?

The answer should have been a resounding *no*. I should have hated him. But I didn't. Not even close.

It had to be the blood bond making me feel this way, but truth be told, I was growing kinda fond of the big oaf. I know. I know. I was out of my mind, but of the creatures I'd met since I got to Hell, Discord was the most...human. He had real emotions, and while he didn't express them much, I got the feeling he might even be a little bit melancholy. Handsome, brooding men were always hard for me to resist...no matter what their species, it seemed.

The seer returned with a small vial and the stack of cash. She fanned it, smiling with the good side of her face as if she'd just won the lottery. Okay, maybe she was a little human too.

"How is he?" I rasped, my lips barely moving as I spoke.

"Oh, he's almost gone." She took a tin from a shelf and set the money inside.

"Please, can you help him first?"

"No."

"Why not? You said he showed you kindness. You can't let him die."

"Death has a different meaning here. It's much more final." She waved her hand over the cauldron and whispered an incantation.

"I know. Discord told me, which is why you need to understand...if he dies, I'll die too." My throat thickened, and if my face wasn't ninety percent frozen, tears might've gathered on my lower lids.

"If you live, he'll live too." She used a ladle to scoop liquid into a mug.

"But for me to live, he has to not die." For being some all-knowing prophet, she sure was dense. I attempted to elaborate on our predicament, but my mouth froze completely. My eyelids followed mid-blink, leaving me looking at the half-witch, half-demon through slits as she worked whatever kind of magic on me she wanted.

That sounded like a fun time, didn't it?

She lifted my torn sleeve and poured her potion into my wound. It sizzled, and searing pain sliced through my shoulder as if she'd dug both hands into the cut and ripped it apart. She hadn't, of course, but she might as well have. My sluggish heart beat excruciatingly hard, and the entire room cartwheeled around me. My vision tunneled, and white sparkles danced around the periphery.

Even if she could get all the poison out of me, I might not survive her healing session.

My head throbbed, and as she chanted in that weird, ancient tongue, my blood turned to lava in my veins, hotter than any witch fire could ever dream to be. My muscles seized, and my bones ached. My consciousness teetered on a razor's edge, and a split second before I fell into oblivion, the poison poured from my wound, splattering onto the floor.

"For Hecate's sake. Did you forget I'm not a demon?" Hey, look at that. I'd found my voice.

"Poison is poison." She set the mug on the nightstand. "The removal process is the same no matter who you are."

I pushed onto my elbows, squeezing my eyes shut against the spinning room. "Can you go remove it from Discord now? I don't know where the arrow got him."

She chuckled and padded to the cabinet. "He was never hit."

"Yes, he was. I had to drag him here." I sat up fully and swung my legs over the side of the bed, opening and closing my mouth to work out the soreness in my jaw.

"No, child." She waved her hand over the cauldron again, whispering something before spooning the potion into another mug. "Your blood bond poisoned him. Drink this."

I accepted the mug and sniffed the liquid inside. It smelled bitter like dandelion root, tinged with an unnatural sweetness that couldn't have come from any earthly plant. I curled my lip. "What do you mean the bond poisoned him? How is that possible?"

She folded her hands over her stomach. "You asked for healing. Drink it if you want him to survive."

Instinct told me never to drink a potion when I didn't know what was in it, but seeing as how I needed him to live if I wanted to survive, I didn't have much of a choice. I chugged the contents, grimacing at the bitter-sweet bite of who-knew-what kinds of roots and smacking my lips, scraping my tongue against the roof of my mouth to get rid of the metallic after taste.

Discord groaned from the other room, and I shot to my feet. The sigil on my arm burned, the glowing red deepening to a blackish-crimson hue. A sudden strength surged through my muscles, and my vision sharpened, the colors of my surroundings growing more saturated and intense.

The bone curtain rattled, and my demon stepped into the room. Without thinking, I ran to him, throwing my arms around him and burying my face in his neck. "Oh, thank Hecate you're okay."

"Hmpf." The seer blew a hard breath through her nose. "Hecate had nothing to do with it."

Discord slid his arms around my waist, pulling me closer before cradling the back of my head in his hand. "That was a close call."

Something between a sob and a laugh rolled up from my chest. "Ya think?"

"Thank you, seer." His chest vibrated against mine. "I am in your debt."

"I paid her." I sniffled and pulled away, stepping out of his embrace. "The ashmarks you gave me."

He nodded. "How many?"

"The whole stack."

His brows shot up, and he blinked three times before sliding his gaze to the seer. "Then it seems you are in my debt."

She shrugged one shoulder dismissively. "Hers, really. She paid me."

"Indeed, she did." He focused on me, and every nerve in my body hummed. He must've felt it too because he inhaled deeply, closing his eyes, a slight smile curving his lips as if he reveled in the sensation.

To be honest, I was reveling in it too.

He snapped his eyes open and cut his gaze to the seer, his brows slamming down as his smile slipped into a frown. "What did you do?"

"I saved you both, as she asked." She carried the mugs to the sink and set them down. "It was the only way."

His hands curled into fists at his sides, and he tightened them, staring daggers into her back as she washed the dishes. Neither of them spoke, but the tension between them grew thicker than my great-grandma's infamous oatmeal.

I cleared my throat. "What exactly was in the potion you made me drink?"

She set the mugs on a shelf and turned around. "You're a powerful witch. You tell me."

"I tasted dandelion and maybe some myrrh. Then

there was something sweet and something metallic that I can't name."

"Detoxification and antiseptic. Very good." She nodded her appreciation. "The sweetness was from the berries of stygian bramble. They aid in psychic connections."

"And the metallic?" Discord asked, his jaw tight.

She steepled her fingers. "Why do you ask questions to which you already know the answers?"

He closed his eyes for a long blink and sighed. "The metallic taste came from my blood. Our bond is now complete. We're inseparable."

My mouth dropped open. "What?"

"It was the only way," she said again.

"You made me drink his blood? *Demon* blood?" My head shook of its own volition, as if every cell in my body refused to accept the information. "No. No, no, no. What do you mean inseparable? How am I...? Demon blood drives mortals insane."

"Not when you're already connected by a blood bond," the seer said.

I opened and closed my mouth a few times, trying to wrap my mind around it. "So I'm not going to lose my mind?"

She laughed. "You summoned a prince through a blood ritual, only to vanquish him so you could get into Hell. That ship has sailed, child."

"It isn't funny." I crossed my arms. Powerful

ancient being or not, she didn't get to mock me...even if she was right.

The seer sighed. "Sit down. Both of you."

I looked at Discord, and he nodded before pulling out a chair for me. He dragged another around the table to sit catty-corner, and the seer took the cauldron from the fire and set it in the center before pulling up another chair.

"When the poison entered your bloodstream," she said as she sprinkled dried herbs into the pot, "Discord attempted to heal you through the connection you forged when you summoned him."

I nodded. "Like he has done before. Why didn't it work this time?"

"The poison the archer used is lethal, even for royalty. The stronger the being, the faster it works. When Discord shared himself with you, it grabbed on to his essence and seeped into his psyche. The actual poison never made it into his bloodstream, but the effects were the same because of your bond."

"So the whole frostbite thing, him not being able to move, was some kind of psychosomatic thing?" I backhanded him on the shoulder. "You made me drag you all the way here when it wasn't even real?"

He narrowed his eyes. "It was very real."

"It was indeed real to him." She stirred the pot and tapped the spoon on the rim before setting it on the table. "So real, in fact, that had you not ingested his blood, it would have killed him. Then you would have died, and I would not have held up my end of the bargain."

She leaned forward, folding her arms on the table. "So, I had to do everything within my power to save you, even if that meant completing your blood bond without your consent. I *always* deliver what I promise."

I drummed my fingers on the table, contemplating what she'd said. We already had a blood bond, thanks to my accident. Surely another little blood exchange wasn't that big of a deal, right? It didn't mean I was doomed to be his *beck and call girl* for all eternity... I hoped. Wait...

"But according to Discord, I overpaid you, right? You still owe me a debt."

She leaned back in her chair, gesturing to the cauldron. "Yes. What would you like to see?"

"Where can we find Hecate?" Discord asked.

The seer looked at me. "Is that what you would like to see?"

"Of course it is." He leaned toward me, resting his palms on the table and giving me a warning look that shot straight to my bones. "If we have her location, we can find her, and you can use your silver tongue to convince her to return to Lucifer's court."

A haunting smile played on the seer's lips, the perfect half of a bow on one side, a strained grimace on the other, both of them edged with way too much amusement for my liking. She opened her mouth to speak, but I held up my hand, stopping her. There was an important piece of information neither of them was sharing with me, and I refused to make another move blindly.

"What does completing the blood bond mean? What has changed?"

Her smile widened. Discord fumed.

"I could have you banished to the ninth level for this." His eyes tightened, the green of his irises billowing like a storm.

She laced her fingers together. "You *could* have, were you still in good standing with your king. As an outlaw, you should be thankful I helped either of you at all."

"When my blood touched his skull, that bound us. What's different now?" I fisted my hands, my nails digging into my palms. If one of them didn't answer me soon, I had a dagger ready for each of them.

"Your blood on his skull bound *him* to *you*," the seer said. "When you ingested his blood, it bound *you* to *him*, completing the most sacred of bonds known to demons. A bond even Lucifer himself has never dared forge."

"I did not ask for this." He slammed his hand onto the table. "Seer, you know me too well to believe I would approve..."

She waved him off. "I merely completed the task

she began in order to save both your lives. Fate willed it, and I complied."

I dropped my hands to my thighs, gripping my weapons. "What. Does it. Mean?"

The seer turned her gaze to me, both her eyes turning glassy white, her hair flowing in a nonexistent breeze. "It means, dear earthly witch, that you are now this demon's soul bride."

CHAPTER 16
DISCORD

I stilled, bracing myself for Cinder's hysteria. Her independent nature, tenacity, and wit...the very things that intrigued me most about this woman...were soon to be the reason for her unraveling.

She blinked, her gaze darting back and forth between the seer and me, a mix of incredulousness and disgust widening her eyes and curling her lip. "Excuse me, I'm his *what*?"

The seer grinned, and if she wasn't a supposedly benevolent being, I'd have knocked the smug expression from her face. "You're his soul bride. His life mate. His wife eternally."

"Wife." Cinder nodded, and for a moment, I thought she might accept the union. Then she shot to her feet, knocking her chair over as she stood.

"His wife?" she nearly shrieked. "You finished what I began?"

She shook her head, lifting a finger as if to speak and lowering it again before pacing to the hearth and back to the table. "I didn't form the blood bond on purpose. I battled a hellhound to get his skull, and I was bleeding when I picked it up. That's it. That's how I *began* this bond, but you knew that, didn't you? You knew it was an accident, and you went ahead and finished it anyway."

"Must I remind you that you would both be dead otherwise?" The seer stood and tucked her chair beneath the table, the demonic side of her voice overpowering the witch. "You gave no stipulations in your request."

Static electricity gathered around the seer, and I could feel the fire crackling in Cinder's soul as she stepped toward her, sparks gathering on her fingertips. As much as I would have enjoyed watching the two of them battle, I had to put an end to the conflict before my nature added fuel to their growing flames of dissonance.

"Now is not the time for hysterics." I rose and righted Cinder's chair. "I need you both to calm down."

They snapped their heads toward me in unison, both of them narrowing their eyes as if I were the one to blame for their disagreement. For once, I'd had nothing to do with it.

"Never tell a woman to calm down," Cinder said, her expression as icy as Medusa's serpentine stare. Oddly, it stirred something deep inside my soul.

"Indeed. You haven't seen hysterics yet." The seer tilted her head, arching her brow.

I closed my mouth and forced a neutral expression. I'd rather take my chances with the hunters than endure the wrath of two powerful women.

"So you can agree on something," I said against my better judgment.

Cinder licked her lips and nodded, her fiery energy cooling to a simmer. "I suppose."

The seer crossed her arms. "Make your request and leave. I have a succubus on her way for a prenatal exam."

"Hecate," I said.

"No." Cinder held up her arm and gestured to my mark. "Undo this. I get that you had to forge the bond to keep us alive, but now you can reverse it. I can't be married to him. I refuse to be his bride, his soulmate... his anything. I'd rather dig my eyes out with an ice cream scoop."

A strange pang formed in my chest at her words. Was I really that revolting? Did she not share any of the attraction I felt to her?

I furrowed my brow. Attraction or no, Cinder was

right. This union had to be dissolved. I had two more stacks of ashmarks in my pockets. If my witch wanted to free herself from me, who was I to stand in her way? I could pay for Hecate's location.

The seer laughed, half-symphony, half-cacophony. "Only Hera herself can annul a soul bond, and good luck convincing her. She rarely intervenes where fate is involved, and she never makes the journey to Hell."

"But this was forced," Cinder said.

"It would not have taken hold if there wasn't at least a small shred of love between you."

Cinder barked a laugh. "Love? I've known the man all of five minutes, and he's been on my nerves every second of it. Can you believe this?" She looked at me, expecting me to confirm the absurdity of the idea.

I could not. "Love might not be the right word, but I cannot deny I feel something akin to fondness."

She crossed her arms. "Well, it's one-sided then."

"Are you certain you don't have the power to reverse the union? At least the second half of it?" I tugged a stack of ashmarks from my pocket. "For a price, of course."

The seer licked her lips as she eyed the cash. "As much as I would love to take your money, I cannot undo it."

"Show us Hecate then." I returned the bills to my pocket.

"No, that's a waste of money," Cinder said. "I can

scry for her myself. Give me the grimoire he paid you with last time, and we'll be on our way."

"Deals in the Underworld are binding." The seer strolled to a bookshelf and ran her fingers over the grimoire's spine. "The book belongs to me now."

"But it's been in my family for decades." Cinder turned on her persuasive magic, her energy shifting, her aura taking on a regal hue as she straightened her spine and lifted her chin. "Surely a being of your power could scan the pages and take in all its secrets. You won't need to reference it again, so what's the point in keeping it?"

The seer's resolve wavered. She nipped her bottom lip between her teeth and reached for the book, hooking her finger over the top and pulling it from the shelf. Resting her right hand atop the cover, she stroked the embossed fire sigil before flicking her gaze to Cinder.

"Nice try, but as I said, deals in Hell are truly binding." She returned the book to the top shelf. "And before you ask for Hecate again, I have scried and searched every day since she disappeared. If I knew where she was, I'd have talked her into returning centuries ago. Lucifer has been as ornery as a hellcat with a bur in its ass since she left him."

"I noticed," I said. "He blames me."

With the women's tempers settled, I returned to my chair and peered into the cauldron. Green and brown crushed herbs floated atop a clear liquid, appearing as mundane as a peasant's stew.

"Of course he does." The seer sat next to me. "The loss of the amulet was Hecate's last straw. Goddess forbid he take responsibility for everything else that led up to her departure."

"And now there's a price on both our heads." Cinder joined us at the table. "Can you show me where my parents are? They're the reason I came here in the first place."

"Have you not scried for them?" The seer waved her hand over the cauldron. "You seemed certain you could locate Hecate with your magic. Why not your parents?"

"I haven't exactly had the time...or the supplies." She gave me a pointed look.

After Lucifer's game of cat and mouse at dinner, being hunted by those who should be my subjects, and a sudden soul bond with a witch who both intrigued and infuriated me, I had forgotten why this entire ordeal had begun.

"Finding your parents is the least of our concerns. Seer, if you can't find Hecate, at least show me where the amulet is."

"No, I need to find my parents." Cinder glared at me. "I'm the one who overpaid for your life."

"You overpaid with *my* money."

The seer sighed and rose. "You have five minutes to

agree upon your request. After that, the overpayment will suffice for this colossal waste of time." She returned the cauldron to the fire.

Cinder leaned toward me, lowering her voice. "I'm the only reason you aren't still wasting away in your dark prison. I get to decide, and I want to see my parents."

"What good is finding your parents when I'm the only one who can break your family's curse?"

She sucked in a sharp breath, her mouth opening and closing twice before she spoke, "Look, I know you want to find your brothers and the stupid amulet, but my parents are suffering. Let me rescue them, and then I promise I will help you free your brothers."

"Are you forgetting about the price on our heads? The moment we leave this cave, we'll be hunted. I have no doubt the archer who shot you was Seraphine, and she toyed with us like a hellcat plays with a rat before devouring it. Next time she aims, her arrow will pierce your heart."

"She won't get the chance again." She angled toward me, her knee resting against mine. The contact made my abdomen tense, but if it affected her in any way, she hid it well.

"You argue as if you've been bound for centuries. Here." The seer dropped a leather sack onto the table in front of Cinder. "Scrying supplies and a cloaking potion that lasts five full minutes. It's already activated, so either of you can use it. Take it and be gone. My appointment has arrived."

"Fabulous." Cinder glared at me and snatched the pouch before retrieving her backpack and shoving it inside.

"Come in, child." The seer waved her hand in front of the curtain, allowing the pregnant succubus entrance. The bones rattled, and the seer gasped.

I grabbed Cinder's arm, shoving her behind me as Bedlam entered the room. He gripped the back of the succubus's neck with one hand and pressed the tip of a jagged, twelve-inch blade against her distended belly. Tears stained the woman's cheeks, and her lower lip trembled as he positioned her halfway through the curtained opening.

"The seer's property is neutral territory," I said, widening my stance and straightening my spine.

He laughed dryly. "It's only her property if she's alive."

"No!" Cinder darted from behind me as a poison-tipped arrow whizzed through the curtain. She grabbed the seer around the waist, tackling her to the floor, but she was too late. The arrow had pierced the seer's heart.

CHAPTER 17

CINDER

I slammed into the seer with enough force to send us sliding across a slick patch of obsidian. We ended up behind a counter, which shielded us from our hunters' view. Of course, Bedlam or Seraphine could've easily stepped around it and severed both our heads in a heartbeat, but Discord kept them occupied.

"The seer was a neutral party," he said. "You had no right to kill her."

I pulled her into my lap, cradling her head as she rasped in a breath. Ice and black lattice spread from the arrow in her chest, across her shoulders, and up her neck. Her pained expression wrenched my heart. She might've bound my soul to a demon I just met, but I wouldn't wish this death on anyone.

"Tell me what to do," I whispered. "Do you have any of the antidote left?"

"Take what you need," she wheezed. "Find Hecate. Set things right." She coughed, and the ice consumed her, freezing her entire body before she crumbled to dust.

"She aided an outlaw. She had no right to live." Bedlam shoved the succubus to her knees, and I scooted toward the end of the counter to get a better view.

Discord growled. "There are laws. Even Lucifer—"

"There are no rules in this game," Bedlam said. "Lucifer wants your heads by any means necessary."

I rose onto my knees and gently tugged a cabinet door open. Jars and vials of herbs and potions filled the space, and I unzipped my backpack to shove an armful of them inside. What they were I had no clue, but surely, they'd come in handy somehow. My grimoire sat atop a high shelf, sadly out of my reach. If I went for it now, I had no doubt I'd take an arrow to my chest, and that would be the end of me.

"Where's the witch?" Seraphine's voice cut through the room, making my skin crawl.

I slipped my backpack onto my shoulders and buckled it at my waist before gripping a dagger and rising to my feet. Bedlam held the succubus by the hair as she trembled, tears rolling down her cheeks. He'd changed out of his dinner suit and now sported black cargo pants, combat boots, and a gray tank stretched so tightly across his pecs that it would probably rip open if he flexed.

Seraphine wore dark purple from head to toe, and her silver hair glinted in the firelight. She leaned her crossbow against the wall by the entrance and held her empty hands in front of her, a swirl of wind and energy forming between them.

Fabulous. She was an elemental witch too.

But she was *just* a witch. My fire might have zero effect on demons, but it sure as shit could burn her.

"Let the succubus go," Discord said. "She has no skin in this game, and Lucifer will have *your* head if you obliterate an unborn spawn."

Bedlam tried to laugh it off, but a hint of fear flashed in his eyes before he shoved her forward. She landed on her hands and scrambled to her feet before darting down a corridor at the back of the room.

"You didn't have to kill the seer." I dropped my empty hand by my side and ignited a fireball behind the counter.

Seraphine scoffed. "This is Hell. We kill anyone who gets in our way."

"Good to know." I hurled the flames at her head.

She threw up her hands, and the spiraling wind turned into a gust that blasted my fire away, extinguishing it as easily as blowing out a match.

Note to self: Wind puts out fire. I'd have to

remember that if I ever found myself battling another elemental…which hopefully would be never.

Bedlam lunged, his fist slamming into Discord's jaw with a *crack*. Seraphine threw another blast of wind at me. The force knocked me from my feet, and I careened backward, smacking into the wall, my dagger clattering to the ground.

I bent to pick it up, and Seraphine's knee connected with my forehead. Pain exploded in my skull, and my vision swam. I slashed out blindly, nicking her arm. She squealed and backpedaled, smacking against the counter and clutching her biceps.

Gripping my favorite dagger, I sent my magic down my arm, and the blade erupted into flames. "You think freezing to death is bad? Try burning from the inside out."

I lunged, aiming for her heart, but she moved left. I drove it into her shoulder instead. She screamed and jerked the blade out, hurling it against the wall. My flames had cauterized the wound, but they'd also ignited a hatred in her eyes that could have melted the skin from my bones.

Discord threw Bedlam against the wall, pissing him off even more. Yellow smoke gathered around the hunter, and his clothes shredded as he morphed into his demon form. He grew a foot taller, with twisted horns jutting from his head and six-inch talons extending from the tips of his fingers and toes.

Discord grunted, but he didn't transform. Instead, he stepped back, his hand resting on the knife in his belt.

"No weapons," Bedlam snarled. "Fight me in your true form."

My demon inclined his chin. "No."

"No?" Amusement danced in Bedlam's eyes. "I'll pluck your head from your neck like a berry in that form. Fight me like a man."

Seraphine scoffed. "Men are all the same. If that one wasn't so good in bed, I'd have fought him like a woman and obliterated him by now."

"You're right. They are." I held up my hands and laced my words with magic. "There's way too much testosterone in power here. Don't you think it's time the women stepped up?"

"I do, which is why I plan to be the one to deliver your heads to Lucifer." She held her hands in front of her chest, her palms facing each other.

"I hear you, but a man will still be in charge. Even if he did appoint you, a witch, to be his right hand, he'd still be the one controlling you."

Bedlam swung a taloned claw. Discord ducked and feinted left before slamming his fist into his kidney.

Seraphine glanced at the demons. "I'll be royalty.

I'll have the king's ear, and Bedlam will be my prince. I'll be unstoppable."

"Until Lucifer tires of you. One wrong move, and he'll cast you out like he did Discord." I slowly lowered my hand toward my knife. "The only way to truly secure your rule is to take down the patriarchy. Make the men serve you, Lucifer included. I can help."

Discord landed a punch in Bedlam's gut.

Seraphine pursed her lips, her eyes calculating. "How can we do it? We're witches in a demon's world."

I wrapped my fingers around the handle. "With the help of a goddess. Hecate is furious with Lucifer. If we find her, we can convince her—"

"Never!" She flung her arms toward me, and a gust of wind lifted me from the ground, whirling me in circles before she fisted her hands. The air steadied, pressing in on me from all directions, holding me in place with my feet dangling six inches from the floor.

"I will never seek the help of that treacherous goddess again." Keeping one hand tightly fisted, she splayed the fingers of her other hand and curled them into a clawlike gesture. "I'll kill you for speaking her name."

I attempted to suck in a breath, but the air around me turned solid, like a block of concrete pressing against my nose. My pulse sprinted, nausea churning in my gut as the panic set in. I couldn't move, couldn't breathe, and as Seraphine tightened her claw, what little air that was left in my lungs rushed out through my nose.

My vision tunneled until all I could see was the sheen of her hair and the smirk on her lips. A flash of light passed across her face. Silver. A blade. Growls rumbled to my right. Discord roared. The blade turned horizontal, getting closer...closer. Cold steel pressed against my neck.

The world went black.

CHAPTER 18

CINDER

My hands scraped across stone, and my chin smacked the ground, rattling my teeth. I scrambled to my knees and crawled forward, my muscles trembling, my stomach heaving. My dinner splattered into the river and floated away.

"Is this water?" I reached for it, ready to scoop it into my arid mouth, but Discord caught my wrist.

"Unless you wish to forget who you are and why you're here, you shouldn't drink from the river Lethe," he said. "Come. We must keep moving."

I sat back on my heels and wiped my mouth with the back of my hand. "Give me a minute."

"We don't have a minute." He hauled me to my feet.

My lungs burned, and my head throbbed. "I just had all the air sucked from my body. Excuse me if I'm not ready to take off in a sprint. Plus, you did your space-bendy thing, which you said could kill me. Thanks for risking my life."

"You'd be dead if I hadn't. Now, we must keep moving. That kind of magic leaves a trail. It won't be long before they find us if we remain here." He clutched my shoulders, sympathy softening his eyes. "I can carry you."

I opened my mouth to protest, to remind him I wasn't some damsel in distress, but the look in his eyes gave me pause. Real concern permeated his expression, and my body drifted toward him of its own accord. He'd saved my life. Again. Between that and the blood/soul bond, it was only natural for me to feel warm fuzzies for the man, right?

It didn't mean I needed to act on it.

"I can walk." I stepped backward, out of his embrace. "What's the plan?"

He cleared his throat. "There's a town just beyond that hill. We can catch a train to the Canyon of Cries and pay cash for a room. There, we will regroup, and you can use the seer's supplies to scry for Hecate."

"What's the Canyon of Cries? Is it like the Grand Canyon of the Underworld?" I adjusted the straps of my backpack and headed in the direction he pointed. "Vacation Central for demons?"

"Something like that." He winced and clutched his chest.

"Are you okay? Did Bedlam get you?" I moved his hand, expecting to find his shirt torn and claw marks on his skin, but it was unmarred.

"I'm afraid my powers grow weaker by the hour. That feat of space-bending magic taxed me more than anything I've felt before." He continued walking, and I matched his pace.

"Do you think it's because of Lucifer? From when he stripped your title?"

"It could be that, among other things."

"What other things? Slow down. My legs aren't as long as yours." I grabbed his arm, and he slowed his pace.

"We've established that our bond weakens my immunity," he said. "Both the Forest of Suffering Souls and Seraphine's poisoned arrow proved the fact. It's possible I'm feeling your reaction to space-bending travel."

I nipped my bottom lip between my teeth, contemplating his words. "Maybe, but this time wasn't nearly as bad as the first. I didn't pass out."

He glanced at me. "Perhaps our bond is strengthening you while weakening me."

"Hmm. I'm not so sure." I shook my head. "Back at the seer's cave...when you refused to fight in your demon form...you weren't being indignant, were you?

You really couldn't transform, just like you couldn't disguise yourself when we got to your secret hideout."

"Correct."

"That had nothing to do with me."

His mouth tightened. "I suppose not. I'm also no longer in possession of the amulet. Its magic strengthens the power of the bearer tenfold. Perhaps it also absorbs power, and that is why I feel weakened."

The path inclined, and my lungs burned as we trekked uphill. "You think some of your power is trapped inside it?"

"It is a possibility."

"That would explain why Hecate is so pissed. Maybe some of her power is trapped in it too."

His brows shot toward his hairline. "If that is the case, convincing her to return to Lucifer without it is futile."

"We have to try."

"I agree. We have no other option."

We reached the top of the hill, and the town came into view. Rows of single- and two-story buildings lined the street, their façades made of onyx and garnet. A train track ran across the foot of the hill, and Discord took my hand, tugging me toward a patch of gnarled trees as a whistle blew and the familiar *chugga chugga* sound vibrated in the air.

"When the train stops, we'll have to run," he said. "Are you able?"

I rubbed my chest and took a deep breath. "My lungs still hurt, but I'll manage. How about you?"

"I will manage as well." He cut his gaze left and right as the train pulled into the station, its brakes squealing and clanking.

A trail of thick black smoke rose from the engine's chimney, and an open car behind it held a massive mound of coal, like the old-timey earthly trains. Behind that, it pulled four passenger cars and half a dozen box cars.

"Now." Discord took my hand again, and together we darted down the hill.

Thankfully, the passengers boarded and exited the train on the opposite side of the track. If we tried to waltz on with them, we'd certainly be met with the same warm welcome we'd received in the last town, and I was way too exhausted to deal with another mob.

We reached the bottom of the hill and dashed left, away from the passengers, before stopping at the second cargo car. A massive padlock, bigger than my hand, secured the door. Discord pulled on it, apparently trying to break it. When he couldn't, he grunted and paced to the next car. I followed him, peering down the line, but every single one had the same type of lock.

"If I wasn't stuck in this form, I could pick it with a

talon easily." He gripped the lock, tensing every muscle in his body and pulling with all his might.

"I'm sure whoever created those made sure they could withstand demon strength. May I?" I gestured to the lock.

"Please." He let go and stepped away.

I hovered my hands over the lock and called on my vim. This act of magic would only add to my exhaustion, but what choice did I have? "Iron bound and sealed tight, hear my call and yield to my might. By flame and force, I break your core. Unlock, unbar, and open the door."

The lock fell open, and I pulled it off the latch. Discord yanked on the heavy metal door, sliding it open just far enough for us to slip through. Inside was dark and dank, and I lit a fireball in my hand as he closed us in. A stack of boxes sat in one corner, but the rest of the space was empty.

"How long is the ride?" I settled onto the floor, leaning my back against the wall.

"It's hard to say. Time is—"

"Different here. Yeah." I closed my eyes and squeezed the bridge of my nose, willing the impending migraine to go away.

"Your body requires rest." He sat next to me.

I laughed dryly. "Ya think? It also requires food and a shower."

"Those things will be available at our next stop. Once we secure the room, I will stay inside while you acquire the provisions."

"What am I, your personal shopper?" I leaned my head back, and the train began moving, the rhythmic cadence lulling me, making it hard to keep my eyes open.

"Without a disguise, I would be recognized instantly. If we are to spend any amount of time in the canyon, I must remain hidden."

"Mmm..." was all I managed before I drifted off to sleep.

"CINDER?" Discord's deep voice seemed to wrap around me, warming me like a heated blanket on a cold winter night. "Wake up. We've arrived."

I snorted, my head jerking as I returned to consciousness. Apparently, I'd gotten cozy during my nap, because I woke with my cheek resting against Discord's chest, his arm wrapped around me. I blinked a few times as my senses returned, and our cuddled position registered in my brain.

"Sorry." I sat up, cringing at the drool stain on his shirt and wiping my mouth.

He looked down and chuckled. "It's better than shedim guts. There's an outfitter next to the hotel. We should have enough ashmarks left to buy new clothes."

"Still, I'm sorry for using you as a pillow." I clambered to my feet and instinctively offered him a hand up.

"I didn't mind." He accepted my gesture, gripping my hand as he stood. "I was quite comfortable, though you do snore."

His grin made my stomach do a flip-flop, and I was certain by the warmth spreading across my cheeks that I blushed. He stepped closer, still holding on to me and raising our entwined hands to his chest.

He stared so deeply into my eyes, I swear he saw the very core of my being. "You're my soul bride. It's my duty to ensure your comfort."

"Umm..." I swallowed hard and tugged from his grasp. "Yeah. No. You don't have to do that."

I shook my head and backed toward the door, silently berating myself for feeling all these warm fuzzies. I should have balked when he called me his bride. Instead, the word burrowed into my heart, attempting to take up residence.

No way could I let that happen.

"I'm compelled to." He cracked the door open and peered from side to side. "It brings me pleasure, which I have not felt in centuries."

He tugged it open further, and I hightailed it out of the car. My boots thudded on the gravel, and I adjusted my backpack as he slipped out and closed the door behind him.

"Yeah, well…" I tapped my arm and then my temple. "We've got the whole blood thing going on, so…"

"Of course. That must be why." He nodded, though he didn't look convinced, and he took a stack of cash from his pocket. "Give me the invisibility spell and go to the back end of the train and cross the tracks. Hold your head high and act like you belong. Now would be a good time to use your silver tongue if you have enough vim."

I handed him the potion bottle and did a quick vibe check. It seemed my sleepy snuggle session with the demon did, in fact, recharge me enough to make this happen. I took the ashmarks and shoved them into my pocket. "Got it. Not a problem."

"The hotel is the red building, three blocks to the east. Pay for one night. I will meet you there." He turned and walked in the opposite direction he had just told me to go.

Watching him walk away sent a flush of panic through my system. My pulse quickened, and my breaths shallowed. I started to call after him, the question of *wait, you aren't coming with me?* on the tip of my tongue.

Get a grip, Cin. I took a deep breath and headed toward the back of the train. I could do this. All I had to do was exude confidence, act like a demon, and pretend I belonged. The confidence part would be no problem. My magic would take care of that. Acting like a demon, though?

"I guess I'll wing it." I reached the caboose and darted across the tracks.

When I joked about this place being vacation central for demons, I had no idea how on the nose I was. Shops and restaurants, bars and luxury hotels stretched down the streets as far as I could see. Demons milled about, some in human form, some not. If we weren't on a timeline...or being hunted...I could have watched and studied them for hours.

Instead, I looked straight ahead, my gaze trained on the small red building on the edge of town. Behind it, mountains towered toward the orange sky, but no snow capped their rocky peaks. Did they even have seasons in Hell? Hopefully, I wouldn't be here long enough to find out.

I strode down the street, away from the crowd, and stopped in front of what Discord had called our "hotel." Aside from being made of stone and glass like every other building around, the place screamed "seedy motel."

The sign above the lobby door hung lopsided, the chain holding it to the roof rusted and broken. Two long buildings stretched out behind it, and I spotted a demon with red skin and three breasts—two nipples on each—walking out of a room and counting a bundle of cash.

Lovely. Discord, my supposed husband, had brought me to a no-tell motel. How romantic.

I squared my shoulders, took a deep breath, and headed for the door. Bones rattled from a mobile above it, signaling my entrance, but the demon behind the counter didn't bother looking up. He had tusks jutting from his top and bottom teeth, and a single horn rose from the center of his head. He leaned his meaty arms on the counter and stared at a small screen that looked an awful lot like a television, and... Was he watching a cooking show?

Hell was so weird. Fire and brimstone here, modern cities there. I don't know what I expected to find when I got to the Underworld, but this definitely was not it.

I started to say excuse me, but I thought better of it. So far, pleasantries and common courtesy didn't seem important in this realm. Instead, I strode to the counter and slapped my hand on the surface.

"I need a room. A clean one," I said.

The demon turned his bored gaze toward me, flicking it to my hand. I glanced down as well and jerked my arm to my side. *Crap!* My shirt had short sleeves, and Discord's sigil was emblazoned across the arm I'd slammed in front of him. Way to put my predicament on display.

If he noticed, he didn't let on. He just grabbed a key from the wall behind him and tossed it onto the counter. "Cleanest one we got. Costs one-eighty for an hour, four-fifty for the night."

"I need it for the night." Doing my best to keep my arm turned so he didn't see Discord's mark, I fished the wad of cash from my pocket and froze. The only writing on the bills was in sigils, and I didn't know how to read demon. I flipped through them, staring at the designs and willing the symbols to speak to me. They didn't, of course, so I laid one on the counter and grabbed the key.

The demon slammed his three-fingered hand onto mine. "I said four-fifty for the night."

I left the key where it was and slid my hand from beneath his before laying another ashmark on the counter. He made a gimme motion, so I laid down a third.

"This ain't a negotiation. Four-fifty or move along." Mucus dripped from his nose, and he wiped it with the same hand he'd used to grab me. *Ick.*

I forced a neutral expression and laid two more bills on the counter. The demon picked up the money, so I snatched the key and strode out the door. I needed a scalding shower and a soak in a tub of hand sani-tizer, stat.

I matched the design on the key to the right door and slid it into the lock. The second I stepped inside,

Discord appeared in the doorway. I gasped, nearly choking on my own heart as he casually stepped inside and closed the door.

"Where have you been?" I took off my backpack and set it on a table.

"Hiding." He rubbed his forehead like he had a headache.

"Did you sprint here? It was definitely more than a five-minute walk." I rested a hand on his shoulder. "Are you okay?

"Yes." He squeezed his eyes shut before opening them again and blinking, his vision seeming unfocused.

"Are you sure?" I leaned in, trying to catch his gaze.

"Yes." He finally looked at me. "The seer's magic didn't agree with me, but I'll recover. Did you have any trouble with the room?"

"Aside from the fact I have no idea how to read ashmarks? No." I cringed. "Well..."

"Well?" He laid four ashmarks on the dresser and pointed at each. "Ten, twenty, fifty, one hundred. What problem did you encounter?"

The little shit in the lobby overcharged me by fifty ashmarks, but I kept that to myself and held up my arm. "Does everyone in Hell know this mark is yours? Because I'm pretty sure the rhinoceros behind the counter saw it."

Discord's brow slammed down over his eyes. "Did he, or didn't he?"

A knock sounded on the door, followed by the rhino's gruff voice. "Housekeeping. I got the towels you wanted."

I clicked my tongue. "Since I didn't ask for any towels, I'm going with *he did*."

CHAPTER 19

DISCORD

I retrieved a dagger from my thigh holster, the worn leather handle rough against my fingers as I clutched it. Without another word, Cinder unzipped her pack and brandished a hunting knife. She nodded once and crept toward the door, positioning herself on the hinged side and resting her hand on the knob.

I understood her plan as plainly as if she'd spoken it aloud.

The brontaur Cinder had encountered in the lobby knocked again. Keys jingled near the lock, and I widened my stance. She mouthed the countdown—*three, two, one*—and flung open the door.

The brontaur snapped his head up. I grabbed his horn and yanked him downward, jabbing my blade into his stomach at the same time. He wheezed and dropped to his knees.

"Did you tell anyone we're here?" Cinder took his horn and turned his head toward her. The brontaur simply grunted in return.

"Answer her." I removed my dagger from his gut, and black blood poured from his mouth.

"Please," he sputtered. "Don't kill me."

"Did you tell anyone?" Cinder asked again.

"No. No." Mucus dripped from his snout.

"Let's keep it that way." Cinder plunged her knife into his chest and twisted it. The brontaur wheezed a final breath before his body and blood turned into ashes.

My heart warmed, and I couldn't fight my smile. "You obliterated him."

"He was planning to do the same to us, and I have way too many unchecked boxes on my to-do list for that." She opened a closet door and retrieved a broom. "Do you think he lied about not telling anyone else?"

I stepped to the side as she swept the ashes out the door. "I believe he spoke the truth. Brontaurs are known for their greed. He wouldn't have risked sharing the bounty."

"Good. That means I have time for a shower." She continued sweeping until the floor was as clean as possible in a place like this.

I watched her intently, my fondness for her growing stronger as she swept away the last of our would-be assassin's ashes. She wasn't using her persuasive magic, yet she exuded calmness and confidence as if battling demons and cleaning up the mess were everyday occurrences. Perhaps in her realm they were.

"What are you grinning about?" She closed the door and returned the broom to the closet.

"You are unlike any woman I have ever met."

She pulled a questioning face. "Thanks? Or was that not a compliment?"

"It was indeed a compliment. You never cease to amaze me." My chest tightened, the idea of keeping Cinder as my soul bride taking root deep within my heart.

She laughed. "Well, then. For my next trick, I guess I'll figure out a way to hide your sigil so I can go into town and buy supplies."

She rummaged through her bag, removing the jars of herbs and spells she'd taken from the seer's abode and setting them on the table. "If Seraphine hadn't decided to suck the life out of me, I could have grabbed my grimoire. It had a good masking spell in it that would have hidden your mark perfectly."

She sank into a chair and examined her loot. "Let me see if I can throw something together."

"There is an easier way." I unbuttoned my shirt and slipped it off before offering it to her. "Here. Save your vim and wear long sleeves."

She accepted the garment and rose to her feet, her gaze wandering down my chest before she looked into my eyes. Her tongue slipped out to moisten her lips, and my stomach tightened. She felt the attraction, the heat building between us. I was sure of it. Her pupils dilated, and her pheromones flared to life as she slipped her arms into the sleeves.

"Thank you." She fastened the top three buttons and gathered the rest of my shirt into her hands, tying it into a knot at her navel.

Blood rushed to my groin. Something about my clothing wrapped around her stirred a deep, primal need inside me. I fisted my hands lest I give in to the urge to wrap *myself* around her.

She cleared her throat and took the ashmarks I had laid out. "Ten, twenty, fifty, one hundred, right?"

"Correct." I breathed slowly and deeply, willing myself to maintain control despite every fiber of my being insisting we consummate our union.

"Clothes, food, weapons if I can find them. I don't suppose there are any swordsmiths in this tourist trap?" She shoved the money into one pocket, the room key into the other.

"I'm afraid not."

"All right. See you soon." She hesitated, her gaze

sweeping over me, caressing me, before she walked out the door.

As it clicked shut behind her, I let out a long, slow breath. *Lucifer, have mercy.* That woman would either be my salvation or my undoing. As long as she was mine, I didn't care which.

I locked the door and kicked off my shoes, laying my clothing on the back of a chair before heading to the bathroom. If I had opted for a higher-end hotel, the faucet would have come with a chiller. Beelzebub knew I needed a cold shower after seeing her reaction to my body.

But I had chosen this place both for its secluded location and its discretion, rather than its amenities. Scalding hot would have to do.

I stepped beneath the stream, allowing the water to soak my hair and roll down my face. I closed my eyes, hoping to enjoy the sensation while focusing on a plan, but my thoughts drifted to the pink-haired beauty who fought like a warrior and negotiated like a royal.

Cinder was smart, quick-witted, confident, and strong. Even without our blood bond, I couldn't deny her qualities. The more I got to know her, the more beautiful she became, and I doubted I could have denied the attraction, whether we were bound or not.

I washed my hair and lathered my body, imagining my hands were Cinder's as I ran them across my chest and down my stomach. Her fingers would feel as soft as velvet against my skin, and the scent of her desire would enrapture me.

My dick throbbed as an image formed in my mind. Her supple curves pressed against me, her hair spilling around me as she gazed into my eyes. I groaned and grasped my cock, stroking it with a soapy hand and imagining Cinder sitting atop me, her center wrapped around me, squeezing me as she moved her hips.

Tightening my grip, I moved my hand faster, stroking from base to tip until my core tightened, winding like a coil, every muscle in my body tensing and then releasing in a rush of ecstasy.

I leaned a hand against the wall, letting the water pelt my flesh as my breathing slowed. When I recovered, I shut off the water and dried myself before wrapping the towel around my waist.

Cinder returned sometime later, her arms full of bags from her shopping adventure. "No one seemed to recognize me, so I guess that's good."

I took one from her and set it on the table. She unloaded the rest before finally looking at me. She sucked in a small gasp, her lips parting slightly and remaining that way as she took in my state of undress.

I chuckled. "Do you like what you see?"

She blinked three times and shook her head. "That's irrelevant. Here."

She pressed a shopping bag against my chest and

sidestepped around me. "I'm going to take a shower, and then we'll figure out our next steps."

"Would you like me to wash your back?" I arched a teasing brow, and she blushed, fighting a smile.

"As tempting as that is, I'll pass." She stepped into the bathroom and locked the door.

CHAPTER 20
CINDER

Discord was fully clothed by the time I finished my shower, and thank the goddess for that. If I'd had to look at those ripped abs and perfect pecs for a moment longer, I would've had no choice but to take him up on his offer to wash my back, my front, and everything else.

He lay stretched out on the bed, his hands folded behind his head, his eyes closed. He looked peaceful... serene...which was weird as all get out considering who he was.

Discord.

His name literally meant disagreement, conflict, strife. Yet, as he lay there quietly, his chest rising and falling rhythmically with his breaths, all I wanted to do was crawl into the bed, curl up next to him, and fall asleep with my head on his shoulder.

It was absolutely bonkers. I knew.

Still, the man had much more depth of character than I ever expected a demon could possess. The little glimpses of vulnerability he'd shown me—like the fact he had a secret hideout for when he got overwhelmed—only endeared him to me more. I couldn't imagine the pain he must be enduring after getting kicked out of the palace. Lucifer's prime predator turned prey.

He sucked in a sharp breath and opened his eyes, his gaze locking on me. His pupils constricted, and he sat up so quickly, my heart leaped into my throat.

"I normally don't require sleep in this realm." He moved to the foot of the bed and pulled on his boots.

"There's nothing normal about any of this." Especially my warm and fuzzy feelings for a demon. *Oof.* "Did you eat?"

"I did not."

"Here. I have no idea what it is, but it looked like a burrito so I grabbed it." I handed him a thin piece of bumpy bread wrapped around some kind of meat with arugula and a brown sauce. "Please tell me that's not a paste of pity and purgatory."

"No, it's a sauce of severed sinuses." He unwrapped the roll and took a bite.

I was about to dig in, but his comment stopped me mid-bite. "For real?"

He laughed and took another bite.

I set mine on the table and opened a bottle of

water. It was glass, of course, because plastic would melt in the Underworld. "What's in it? Actually, what is this? I don't want to drink the tears of the tormented."

"Such things are delicacies found only in Lucifer's palace. You purchased water and roasted beef, though the shape and texture of the bread are unfamiliar."

"We call them wraps in my realm." I took a sip of water. It had a hint of rotten egg smell, but I supposed that was normal for his realm.

"Wraps." He nodded thoughtfully. "An appropriate name."

We finished our food in silence, and I choked down the whole bottle of stinky water because hydration seemed extra important in Hell for some reason. Then I gathered the trash and stuffed it into the bin before taking stock of my magical supplies.

I opened the leather pouch the seer had given me and emptied the contents onto the bed: Two red candles, a sachet of herbs, a few bone fragments— from what creature, I did not want to know—and an obsidian pendulum hanging from a chain made of pointy teeth.

I pressed the sachet of herbs to my nose as I sank onto the mattress. The scents of sage and wormwood, bitter and pungent, were unmistakable.

"Oh, sweet spirits." I wrinkled my nose and dropped the pouch next to the other items. "I don't know how the seer scried with this stuff, nor do I want to find out. I'm a light witch. Aside from the candles, this stuff is useless. She didn't even give me a bowl."

"How does a light witch scry?" He picked up the pouch and gave it a whiff, curling his lip as if the odor offended him.

"Not with dead things." I paced to the sink and filled a stone mug with water. "If she'd given me pure sage, I could've burned it to cleanse the space. I'd choke on the stench if I tried burning wormwood."

"I'm surprised her demonic side didn't recoil at the use of sage." He lifted the pendulum, running his fingers over the strung teeth. "That foul herb is not native to this realm. I can only imagine the demon who brought it to her must've requested a taxing favor."

I cleared the table, moving everything but the mug and the candles to the bed. "It's valuable then."

"Exceedingly rare."

"Considering the amount I paid her, I suppose it makes sense then." I set the candles on either side of the mug and shot a flame to each wick, lighting them before peeking out the window to be sure "housekeeping" wasn't on the way with more towels.

"Scrying puts me into a trance. I'll be vulnerable while I'm under, so please stay awake and alert." I settled into a chair and rested my palms on the table.

"I won't let any harm come to you." The conviction

in his voice sent a warm shiver up my spine, and he moved to the side of the bed facing me and sat up straight, resting his hands in his lap.

I inhaled deeply, preparing to center myself, but the overwhelming scent of the candles gave me pause. "Why do they smell like bacon?"

"They're made from tallow, rendered fat from the elysian boar."

"Tasty. If only I had a spoon."

"I wouldn't recommend consuming them. Their scent may be appetizing, but their taste is quite bitter."

I thought about asking how he knew, but nah... I'd rather not know all his kinks. Not yet anyway.

I shook my head, chasing away *that* thought, and focused on the flames. They flickered in response to the magic building in the core of my being, my own fire growing, heating me from the inside out. I relaxed my eyes, allowing my vision to blur, the flames getting fuzzier until soft orange light encircled my view of the water in the mug.

"Hear me, Hecate, and heed my call. Aid me in my search for...well, for you." I stared into the mug, allowing my senses to slip away. "I am your faithful disciple, and I need your aid. Show me where you are."

I took another deep breath. Two. Three. My body relaxed until I felt as if I were floating in the ether. I focused on the goddess, willing her to reveal her location, finding nothing but emptiness in my trance.

"If not your location, please show me my parents." I waited, focusing, sifting through the ether as if panning for gold. I might as well have been searching inside a vacuum.

With another deep breath, I returned my attention to my senses and the world around me. I blinked my vision into focus and rubbed my temples. "That's weird. I found nothing. Not even a shred of a hint."

"Hecate does not wish to be found."

"Maybe not, but my parents sure as shit do. Let me try again." I returned my palms to the table.

"Does scrying not tax your vim?" he asked.

"It does, but it's better than being obliterated."

He took the chair across from me and set the seer's supplies on the table. "There is a saying from long before your time. 'When in Rome...'"

"Do as the Romans do." I crossed my arms.

"You know it?"

"Everyone does."

"Perhaps these items are required for scrying in this realm." He pushed the herb sachet and pendulum toward me.

I let out a slow breath and eyed the bone fragments lying next to the pendulum. He had a point. Dark magic and low vibrations penetrated every atom in this realm. The very air I breathed was thick and heavy with power. My light magic couldn't penetrate the darkness here.

I scooped the bones into my hand and dropped them into the mug. "She could've at least given me directions."

I opened the pouch and dumped the bitter herbs in with the bones. Discord made a disgusted face that I was certain matched mine, and I picked up the dental pendulum, swirling it over the water. "Does she usually recite an incantation when she scries?"

"Yes, but it's dependent on what she's looking for. Her words change every time."

"I suppose I can make one up on the fly." I stared into the mug. The bones had sunk the moment I dropped them in, but the sage and wormwood floated on the surface as if I were seasoning a broth. I suppose I sort of was.

"Hear me, Hecate, and heed my call. Reveal your location and save us all." I zoned out again, allowing my consciousness to slip into the ether, but still, I only found emptiness.

"My mother and father are trapped in this realm. Give me sight to resolve my plight." I waited and searched. My stomach clenched, and sharp pain shot to my temple, reminding me not to grit my teeth.

Another moment or two passed before I blew out a hard breath. "Nothing. Again. Wait..."

I looked at Discord, who sat patiently across from me, his hands resting atop the table. "The seer was half-demon, half-witch, right?" I asked, and he nodded.

"This is demon territory. Maybe I can't see into the ether here because I'm all witch."

He raised his brows. "That's a strong possibility."

I reached for his hand across the table and clutched it in mine. His skin was warm and soft, and he held me back as if his hands were made to hold me. "Can you share your energy with me? If I can channel some of your demonicness, maybe I can mix it with my witchiness and break through."

"That could work." He nodded in appreciation. "You are as clever as you are beautiful."

My stupid cheeks heated at his words, so I angled my head down and stared into the mug. "Let me have it."

My palm tingled where we touched. Then, heat spread through my hand and spiraled up my arm before flowing into my chest and filling me with more power than any witch should possess. I gasped, the sensation both exhilarating and terrifying at the same time.

His magic didn't scare me. In fact, it felt...right. That was the frightening part because I could *so* get used to the feeling. My nerves fired on overdrive, connecting in ways they never had before, and my skin turned to gooseflesh, my senses heightening as his essence surged through me.

I recited another incantation and took a deep breath as Discord's energy danced with mine, swirling and melding until I couldn't tell where mine ended and his began.

We were one being in that moment, and I'd be lying if I said it wasn't the first time in my life I'd felt completely whole. But I could ponder the unnatural rightness of channeling this demon later.

I slipped into the ether, and this time it wasn't empty. I couldn't see the goddess, but I felt her in my soul. Digging in deeper, I focused on the surroundings in my vision. "Fire, brimstone, a cave, and a crumbling temple."

"Is Hecate there?" Discord's voice sounded miles away.

"Yes. No. I can't see her, but I feel her." My brow furrowed as I concentrated on the goddess. "There's a shroud."

"Look for details," he said. "There are hundreds of crumbling temples in this realm."

I shifted my focus away from the being and turned to the temple in my mind. Three Corinthian columns stood at the front of the stone structure, their capitals adorned with acanthus leaves and skulls. Three steps led up to the entrance, an archway with the triple moon symbol carved above the door.

"It's a temple for Hecate." I described it to Discord. "She's hiding out in her own temple."

"The last place anyone would think to look."

"They wouldn't find her even if they did. She's the goddess of magic. Her shroud is strong."

"I know the location." He started to tug from my grasp, but I held him tighter.

"I need to look for my parents while I'm under." I left the temple in my mind and focused on my mother's energy. It was there, teasing the outskirts of my vision, her high vibration contrasting with the low hum of the Underworld.

A commotion sounded outside, and Discord tightened his grip on my hand. "Wake up, Cinder. We must leave."

"Not until I find my parents." I squeezed my eyes shut, trying my damnedest to stay inside the trance.

"Now." He swiped the mug and everything else from the table, yanking me back into the present.

"What the hell?" I stomped on a candle that was still lit. "I was so close."

"So are they." He moved the curtain aside, and I caught a glimpse of silver hair at the front of the property. Seraphine had found us.

"Well, shit."

CHAPTER 21

CINDER

"Think you'll fit through the window?" I shoved everything into my backpack and slipped my arms through the straps, buckling it at my waist before pacing toward the bathroom.

"I think I have no choice." Discord followed, and I pried open the pane.

"How did they find us?" I stepped onto the back of the toilet and braced my hands on either side of the window before pulling myself up onto the ledge. A quick glance left and right said the coast was clear for now, so I hopped out, my boots thudding on the rocky ground.

"Bedlam is an excellent tracker. Apparently, Seraphine is as well." He narrowed his eyes at the window. There was no way he'd fit through, so he did what any big, burly demon would do and yanked it from the wall. The glass cracked, and he tossed it aside before climbing out to join me.

"Fabulous," I said. "How do we get to the temple?"

"The quickest way is to cross the canyon. Come." He hung a left and strode toward the back of the property.

I jogged to keep up—no more scurrying...*yay*--and we scaled a chain link fence before darting into the trees. We reached a clearing, and the massive canyon stretched out before us. A steaming stream of green-ish-yellow liquid flowed through the bottom, having etched into the volcanic rock for millennia upon millennia, creating ledges and crevices in the mile-deep ravine.

To our right, a visitor center stood in the distance, with an obsidian bridge stretching across a narrower section of the canyon. To our left lay nothing but miles and miles of rocky terrain.

We went left—because of course we did—running along the ridge until my lungs burned and my legs ached.

"Where can we cross?" I panted and slowed my pace.

"A mile ahead," he said, and he jerked his head toward something behind me. "Quickly."

He grabbed my hand and pulled me down a narrow path, into the ravine. My boot slipped on the gravel, and I fell, my left leg folding beneath me as I rolled and slid deeper and deeper into the canyon.

"I suppose that's one way to do it." Discord leaned back, steadying himself with his hand and allowing the gravel to carry him down to my side.

I landed on a ledge with a grunt and unfolded my legs. Sitting up, I clutched my head and squinted against the orange moonlight. Two silhouettes passed above us before disappearing from view.

I stumbled to my feet, gripping the rocks on the side of the canyon, lest my dizziness send me plummeting into the acidic liquid below. "Those two just won't give up."

"Not until we're dead. Come." He took my hand, and we scooted along the ledge, our backsides pressed against the wall.

I held my breath as I crossed a narrow section of the path, my toes hanging over the edge. My pulse sprinted, and I swallowed the bitter taste in my mouth. "How about we kill them first?"

"That would be an excellent plan if we had more weapons." He dropped my hand and leaped onto a shelf in the rock. I followed.

"We do. Check my pack. The blue bag." I turned my back toward him, and he unzipped it to retrieve the set I'd picked up at the outfitters.

"Camping knives against poisoned arrows and air

magic." He frowned and handed me two from the set. "I don't like our odds."

I shoved them both into my thigh holster. "You sound more worried about Seraphine than Bedlam."

"I will never underestimate the abilities of a witch again."

"Smart man." I started for a trail leading deeper into the ravine.

A slight shift in the wind signaled Seraphine's presence, and my instincts kicked in. I ducked a fraction of a second before the first arrow whizzed past my head. Straightening, I hurled a fireball the size of a watermelon, but she turned her palm up and rose from the ground, levitating.

A tiny tornado swirled around her feet as she floated over the ravine and descended. She attached her crossbow to her back and shoved her hands toward us. Wind blasted us backward. Discord caught himself on a piece of jagged rock, but I tumbled over the ledge.

I had never fallen from anything higher than two stories, which only gave me enough time to think *oh, shit* before I hit the ground. With the bottom of the ravine five thousand feet below, I had plenty of time to contemplate my life choices before my body went splat.

Maybe I should have enlisted my sisters' help in this adventure. Hecate knew I could use one of Ash's on-the-fly spells. A massive pillow of air to bounce off of would have been nice. Instead, it looked like I'd find out exactly what that greenish-yellow liquid flowing through the canyon was made of.

I was just about to kiss my life goodbye when an invisible cord stopped me mid-air. My body folded as if a rope were wrapped around my waist, and my neck snapped back and forward with enough force to give me whiplash.

I spun, rolling over and over like a gas station hot dog. Seraphine stood at the bottom of the canyon, a maniacal grin stretching across her face as she toyed with me. Discord stood on a ledge a few yards up, he and Bedlam both wielding knives and glowering at each other.

I kept spinning, circling, circling, circling. If Seraphine didn't stop me soon, she'd have to deal with a vomit cyclone.

I chunked a fireball at her, but my aim was off, thanks to the spin cycle. It hit the stream, and a geyser of putrid liquid shot twenty feet high before raining onto her. She squealed, her skin sizzling as the droplets hit her, the distraction enough to make her lose her grip on me.

Acid rain wasn't what I'd been going for, but the end result worked out just fine...ish. I fell the remaining ten feet, my body crumpling with the impact, but I managed to right myself and face her like the strong elemental witch I was.

Her eye twitched as her burns healed. Apparently, Lucifer had granted her a speed-healing ability when he'd dragged her from the pits of despair. Fabulous.

"You don't have to do this. I'm not a threat to you." I raised my hands and activated my persuasion magic. "I have no desire to join Lucifer's court. I swear."

She blinked, my magic making her consider my words. "Then why are you here?"

"I came to rescue my parents. A demon tricked them. I just want to take them home."

Seraphine laughed, and I glanced up at the commotion of the warring demons above. Discord jabbed a knife into Bedlam's gut, but the hunter shoved him, pushing him over the edge. He tumbled down, landing on another shelf ten feet above us.

"Why is that funny?" I asked, keeping her focus on me.

"Because you can't escape Hell. No mortal can." She looked at me like I'd grown a second head.

"Right. Not without Lucifer's blessing, but I'm sure Hec—" I stopped myself from finishing the goddess's name. Mentioning her nearly got me killed last time. "I'm sure he'll give it to me. I can be very persuasive."

She laughed harder. "Even if you could persuade him, he literally can't help you. Not without the amulet that your boyfriend lost." She reached behind her back for her crossbow.

"What do you mean?" I laid my magic on as thickly as possible, demanding she return her full attention to me. "What does the amulet have to do with it?"

"If I tell you, I'll have to kill you."

"Aren't you planning to do that anyway?" My muscles tightened, and I shifted my weight, preparing to either attack or run. I wasn't sure which.

She notched an arrow and pulled back the string. "He demanded a sacrifice from Hecate to prove her devotion, so she demanded one from him."

"Eyes on me," I said, daring to push my magic further into the gray. "What did they sacrifice?"

She snapped her gaze to mine, unable to fight my command. "Lucifer gave up the ability to send beings across the veil. The only way a creature from this realm can cross is if they are summoned. Weaker entities can still slip through rifts, but he can no longer send anyone...including a witch...to the other side."

My stomach sank. "And Hecate?"

Her lip curled. "She gave up her power of resurrection, promising never to take a soul from Lucifer's domain. Both their powers now reside in the amulet. Without it, you're stuck here, and I'm not about to give up my chance at the throne."

She lifted her crossbow, and I charged. The arrow

hit my hair, ripping a chunk from the roots before lodging in the wall behind me. She already had another in her hand, ready to reload, when I sank my shoulder into her stomach and tackled her.

The crossbow skidded across the rocks, and the arrow clattered to the ground. She shoved me off and scrambled for it, but I grabbed it first and stood, raising it toward her.

She clambered to her feet. "Hoarfrost isn't poisonous to air witches."

"Maybe not, but arrows still hurt like a mother." I lunged and sank the tip deep into her shoulder.

She stumbled backward and yanked it out, blood spouting from the wound as she chucked it to the ground. "You bitch!"

"Come on now. That's not a very girl power insult." I grabbed a knife from my thigh holster and circled her. "Hit an artery, didn't it? You might want to put pressure on that before you bleed out."

She raised her hands, and a gust of wind whipped toward me. I leaned into it, planting my feet in a wide stance and bracing myself against the assault. As long as she didn't reverse it and suck the life out of me again, I could give her a run for her money.

I plowed forward, a knife in one hand, fire dancing just below the surface of the other. Gravel rained from the ledge above, and Discord grunted, his foot slipping over the edge. Seraphine clapped, and the gale-force wind I was leaning into dissipated in an instant.

I stumbled forward, catching myself on my hands. Skin ripped from my palms, and searing pain pulsed through them. "Son of a banshee!"

Scrambling to my feet, I shot a stream of fire toward her, burning a hole in her shirt and scorching her stomach. She groaned and countered me with wind, pushing my flames toward me until we looked like characters from a video game, equally matched.

"I really don't want to kill you." I strained, pushing my fire harder against her air. "My sisters are on the other side of the veil. They can find the amulet and make things right."

"Right? And give that bitch of a goddess a place by Lucifer's side? Not a chance." She forced the wind toward me, gaining distance in our elemental standoff.

"All I want is to find my parents and go home."

"All I want is your head on a stake."

I glanced at the ledge above. Discord's fist connected with Bedlam's jaw. The hunter lunged, and they both tumbled, landing at our feet with grunts and groans. The distraction was enough for me to dart left, out of the wind stream, and barrel into Seraphine, shoving her with everything I had.

She landed on her butt at the river's edge and scrambled toward the crossbow. Bedlam turned his fingers into talons and slashed at Discord, ripping his stomach open. My demon fell. Bedlam pinned him to the ground.

Seraphine grabbed her crossbow and notched an arrow, aiming at my chest. Bedlam lifted his taloned hand above Discord's chest.

CHAPTER 22

CINDER

I dropped, spinning and kicking out a leg like Ember had taught me. My move knocked Seraphine off balance, and I grabbed the crossbow as she fell, aiming it at Bedlam's heart. He struck out, but before his claws could penetrate Discord's heart, I pierced his with Seraphine's poisoned arrow.

His eyes widened, his jaw falling slack as he clutched the shaft protruding from his chest. Discord shoved him to the ground and rose, his face contorted in pain.

"My demon!" Seraphine jumped to her feet as Bedlam's skin turned the telltale icy blue with black lattice.

She rushed toward him, hatred and fury igniting in

her eyes. I hit her with a fireball, knocking her back. She lifted her hand toward me, making the claw-like gesture she'd used the last time she sucked the air from my lungs.

"Not this time." I drew in a breath and held it.

Discord shot a stream of flames at her chest. I threw a fireball at her head. She staggered backward, falling into the river with a splash.

Seraphine screeched and screamed, flailing in the acid as it ate at her skin. If I'd had another arrow, I would've put her out of her misery. Instead, I stood there watching, my heart aching as she dogpaddled to the opposite side and dragged herself onto the stones. She let out one more agonizing wail before collapsing face down on the rocky bank.

My stomach soured, and my chest ached at the sight of her lying on the riverbank. Never would I ever wish that kind of pain on anyone...even someone trying to kill me.

Bedlam groaned, drawing my attention away from the lump of burned flesh. Ice crept up his neck, and he wheezed as his lungs began to freeze. "She...will avenge me."

I scrunched my nose. "Not in that condition, she won't."

A high-pitched whining noise emanated from his form, and he crumbled into ashes.

I looked at Discord, and he looked back at me, his expression a mix of concern, relief, and admiration all at the same time. We stood there for a bit, locked in each other's gazes, and warmth expanded in my chest, making it ache in a good way.

"I'm okay," I finally said, and I closed the distance between us.

"As am I. It's already healing." He lifted his torn shirt to show me his wound. The edges had begun stitching themselves back together.

We stood a foot apart, his sigil on my arm heating and pulsing in response to...our proximity? Our magic? My desire?

"Looks like we beat the first level of the game." My lips tugged into a smile, and a weird giddy sensation spiraled through my stomach.

"Indeed we did." He reached for my hair, brushing it from my forehead and tucking it behind my ear as he stepped toward me.

The giddy sensation bubbled up to my chest before shooting into my brain and erasing all logical thought from my mind. I slid my hands up his chest, clasping them behind his neck and pressing my lips to his.

He responded, wrapping his arms around my waist and pulling me against him. Cradling the back of my head in his hand, he drank me in. I opened for him, and he brushed his tongue to mine, sending an electric jolt through my entire body.

All my muscles turned to goo, and I leaned into him, allowing myself to get lost in his essence. I fit in his arms as if I were made specifically for his embrace. His lips were soft, the kiss firm and purposeful.

Was I certifiable for standing next to an acid river, making out with a demon? One hundred percent. Did I care? Not right then. Not at all.

I reveled in the warmth of his embrace, wishing the moment would last forever. But you know what they say. All good things must come to an end.

The thing that ended the best kiss of my life? My chest feeling like some magical force was trying to turn me inside-out. I groaned, and he gripped my shoulders, pushing me away.

"Someone is attempting to summon me." Alarm crumpled his brow and widened his eyes at the same time. "I cannot fight the pull."

I heaved in a breath and stumbled, dripping to my knees. "It hurts."

"If they succeed, you won't survive." He kneeled next to me and reached for my face, but his arm turned into green smoke.

I cupped his cheek in my hand and closed my eyes, focusing on our bond, willing, hoping the completed binding ritual would be enough to keep him by my side.

It wasn't.

Smoke crept up his arms, spiraling around his

head, billowing down his body until his entire physical form morphed into a cloud of green. My head throbbed, my skull threatening to split beneath the pressure. I lay on my side, clutching the sigil on my arm as my vision tunneled into blackness.

A bright white light appeared in front of me in my mind. Was this the end? Was my soul being obliterated?

The light flashed, and a vision formed. Ash's studio. She and Ember stood outside a summoning circle with two men.

Chaos and Mayhem.

I recognized them instantly, my bond with Discord not only allowing me to see with his eyes, but to feel his emotions, read his thoughts. In his smokey form, he moved around the perimeter of the circle, first looking at Chaos and then Mayhem.

A spark of hope ignited in my chest, and though my pain tried to extinguish it, I held on to the flame. Ash had found my journal. She and Ember had released Discord's brothers. But the veil...

Even as my body was dying, I could sense the unnatural thinness, could feel the rifts my sisters had mended. All Hallow's Eve was fast approaching, and in its current state, the veil wouldn't survive.

"Ask them for the amulet," I said in my mind, hoping to Hecate that Discord could hear me. *"It has the power of resurrection. I can't go home without it."*

My muscles screamed with pain. My bones were about to splinter and crumble.

"Have you the amulet?" Discord's voice echoed from both sides of the veil.

"We have the means to avenge our imprisonment," Chaos said. "Join us in the mortal realm so we can identify Isabel's descendants and claim our prize."

"I owed a debt to the witch who freed me, and no one else," Discord said, being cryptic AF, as usual.

"Tell them to get the amulet, and then get your ass back over here. I won't last much longer."

"That's our sister, Cinder," Ash said. "She needs you to find our parents and bring them all here to break my family's curse."

He had the nerve to laugh. "That was not the debt she asked I pay."

Okay, this was ridiculous. I got that withholding information to maintain control was kinda Discord's thing, but I was lying there about to die while he played games with our siblings. It was time to pull the plug and bring my demon home.

I focused on the fire symbol etched into his skull and sent a pulse of persuasive magic through his sigil and into his psyche. *"Come back now."*

"I'm trying, but your sisters are strong."

"Our soul bond is stronger. Come back. I need you." I pushed out every ounce of vim in my system and latched on to Discord's essence.

Mayhem stepped toward the circle. "Join us, brother. We have fae to battle."

"*Not now, you don't.*" I imagined my vim digging claws into his soul.

"Find my amulet, and I will consider it," he said before I wrenched him home.

Also by Carrie Pulkinen

Fire Witches of Salem Series

Chaos and Ash

Commanding Chaos

Claiming Chaos

Mayhem and Ember

Mending Mayhem

Mastering Mayhem

Discord and Cinder

Demanding Discord

Desiring Discord

Collection One: Books 1-3

Collection Two: Books 4-6

New Orleans Nocturnes Series

License to Bite

Shift Happens

Life's a Witch

Santa Got Run Over by a Vampire

Finders Reapers

Swipe Right to Bite

Batshift Crazy

Holy Shift

Collection One: Books 1-3

Collection Two: Books 4-7

Crescent City Wolf Pack Series

Werewolves Only

Beneath a Blue Moon

Bound by Blood

A Deal with Death

A Song to Remember

Shifting Fate

Collection One: Books 1-3

Collection Two: Books 4-6

Haunted Ever After Series

Love at First Haunt

Second Chance Spirit

Third Time's a Ghost

Love and Ghosts

Love and Omens

Love and Curses

Collection One: Books 1 - 3

Collection Two: Books 4 - 6

Stand Alone Books

Flipping the Bird

Sign Steal Deliver

Azrael

Lilith

The Rest of Forever

Soul Catchers

Bewitching the Vampire

ABOUT THE AUTHOR

Carrie Pulkinen is a paranormal romance author who has always been fascinated with things that go bump in the night. Of course, when you grow up next door to a cemetery, the dead (and the undead) are hard to ignore. Pair that with her passion for writing and her love of a good happily-ever-after, and becoming a paranormal romance author seems like the only logical career choice.

Before she decided to turn her love of the written word into a career, Carrie spent the first part of her professional life as a high school journalism and yearbook teacher. She loves good chocolate and bad puns, and in her free time, she likes to dance, drink wine, and travel with her family.

Connect with Carrie online:
CarriePulkinen.com